Here Is Not Our Home

A Novel

Here Is Not Our Home

A Novel

By Francis Mallett

Ariadne Press

Riverside, CA

Here Is Not Our Home
By Francis Mallett

New Edition
Published by Ariadne Press
ISBN 978-1-57241-223-1

Cover:
Richard Gerstl: Study of Mathilde Schoenberg 1907
Tempera on canvas, 94x74cms (detail)
Oesterreichische Galerie, Vienna

Publisher's Cataloging-in-Publication data

Names: Mallett, Francis, author.
Title: Here is not our home / by Francis Mallett.
Description: New edition. | Includes bibliographical references. | Riverside, CA: Ariadne Press, 2023.
Identifiers: LCCN: 2023916152 | ISBN: 978-1-57241-223-1
Subjects: LCSH Gerstl, Richard, 1883-1908--Fiction. | Kallir, Otto, 1894-1978--Fiction. | Schoenberg, Arnold, 1874-1951--Fiction. | Schoenberg, Mathilde, 1877-1923--Fiction. | Artists--Fiction. | Vienna (Austria)--History--Fiction. | BISAC FICTION / Biographical | FICTION / Historical / 20th Century / General
Classification: LCC PS3615 .A35 H47 2023 | DDC 813.6--dc23

Ariadne Press | Riverside, California

‘Central Europe between 1900 and the early 1930s- from the publication of Freud’s ‘Interpretation of Dreams’ to Hitler’s rise to power – was truly the smithy in which were forged many of the weapons, both verbal and physical, with which battles over the minds and bodies of men, throughout the world, have been waged ever since.’

Thomas Szasz – ‘Karl Kraus and the Soul-Doctors’.

AUTHOR'S NOTE

In early May 1906 Gustav Mahler conducted a performance of Richard Wagner's Tristan and Isolde at Vienna's Court Opera House. Among those in the audience were composer Arnold Schoenberg, who was on the verge of transforming the history of music, a budding art student from Linz, Adolf Hitler, as well as a totally unknown young painter, Richard Gerstl. All shared an unqualified admiration for Wagner's music. Within that tiny area which comprised central Vienna in those years lived others who would prove to be just as significant in the century's cultural and political history, including Leon Trotsky, Sigmund Freud, architect Adolf Loos, film maker Fritz Lang and philosopher Ludwig Wittgenstein. Gerstl's personal circumstances meant not only that his belated claim to be part of this group has only been slowly recognised but that his work was very nearly entirely lost to posterity. It was only thanks to the insight of Viennese art dealer Otto Kallir that this didn't happen.

I first encountered Richard Gerstl's work as a student in the mid-1970s in a general book on Expressionism where his 1908 Schönberg Group portrait was illustrated. Its radical nature seemed to me almost inexplicably ahead of its time. I had recently returned from six months at Vienna University but had not come across any of his paintings in the galleries or museums there, while in Britain he was a complete unknown. Biographical information was very scarce. Some 30 years later I discovered there was a collection of his paintings in the new Leopold Museum, and I went back to Vienna to see them. I gradually acquired all the books and catalogues about his work which had been published in the meantime. I had the idea of a book which fused together two things: an account of the life of Richard Gerstl and an exploration of how the philosophical, political and aesthetic ideas which had largely originated in Vienna in that era, were still relevant today. When I started writing the book I had an unformed idea that much of the wider historical events of that period were mirroring unfolding events in the wake of the 2008 financial crash and the ever-growing global rise of nationalism, but by the time I had finished, it had become disconcertingly ever more obvious.

I had collected a wider library on the artists, musicians and thinkers in Vienna of that period, including diaries and letters, which became important sources of information. The most significant are listed below. The groundbreaking books on Gerstl's paintings by art historians Otto Breicha and Klaus Albrecht Schroeder were vital. In more recent years London University's Dr. Raymond Coffer's research and website with previously unseen archive material relating to Gerstl's life have proved an invaluable aid.

I thought initially of constructing the book entirely from existing texts and archive material. A kind of literary ready-made. But it wasn't long before the formal problems inhibited this. Who would or could tell Gerstl's story? What about the missing parts? It eventually became clear that, other than a false omniscient narrator, Otto Kallir was the only possible candidate. His story seemed inextricably linked to Gerstl's own and slowly became just as important. Kallir's interviews with those who had known Gerstl were stories within stories, 'Rahmenerzaehlungen', reminiscent of 19C German Novellen writers such as my particular facourite, Theodor Storm. Inevitably, there remained events which no character could credibly know or tell.

I had come across Joseph Koerner's moving film 'Vienna City of Dreams' and realised that the strange, compelling appeal of Vienna is that most people drawn there were exiles of some kind. It is almost nobody's natural home – literally 'unheimlich' – a kind of metaphor for the human condition in the 20C/early 21 C – whether geographical, political, cultural or existential exile. It reinforced the subconscious significance in the book of the line from Wagner's Wesendonck Lieder – 'Unsere Heimat ist nicht hier'. The idea of the 'unheimlich' or 'uncanny' became part of the inspiration for Smaragda Berg's account of those curious links between early Modernism and Esotericism, strangely mirroring the Occult roots of Nazism. Mathilde Schoenberg's dream, the narrative of Schoenberg's *Erwartung*, foretells the tragic events of Gerstl's death, while the seance brings the traumatic events back from the 'other side' long before the dream is ever revealed. Dreams and memory – we are forever caught between the two.

Many of the ideas about painting, the self-portrait in particular, as well as aesthetics, are indebted to British artist Robert Lenkiewicz (1941–2002).

Francis Mallett
June 2022

SELECTED BIBLIOGRAPHY

Otto Nirenstein (later changed to Otto Kallir), *Beiträge zur Vischerforschung,* Vienna Universitätsarchiv: Diss. 3. Juni 1930, promoviert am 21.03.1931, PN 10749, Schachtel 115.

Alban Berg: Letters to his wife, edited, translated and annotated by Bernard Grün, London: Faber, 1971

Zemlinsky Studies, ed. Michael Frith, London: Middlesex Univ. Press, 2007

Wittgenstein reads Weininger, ed. David G. Stern, Béla Szabados, Cambridge: Cambridge Unv. Press, 2004

Joan Allen Smith, *Schoenberg and His Circle: A Viennese Portrait,* New York: Schirmer, 1986

Marc D. Moskowitz, Alexander Zemlinsky: *A Lyric Symphony,* Woodbridge: Boydell, 2010

Karen Monson, *Alban Berg: A Biography,* London Sydney: Macdonald and Jane's, 1980

Jane Kallir, *Schönberg's Vienna,* New York: Galerie St. Etienne, 1984

Jane Kallir, *Austria's Expressionism,* New York: Galerie St. Etienne, 1981

Patrick Werkner, *Austrian Expressionism: The Formative Years,* Palo Alto: Society for the Promotion of Science and Scholarhip, 1993

Zemlinsky's Briefwechsel mit Schönberg, Webern, Berg und Schreker, ed.

Horst Weber, *Briefwechsel der Wiener Schule Band 1,* Darmstadt: Wissenschaftliche Buchgesellschaft, 1995

Anthony Beaumont, *Zemlinsky,* London: Faber, 2000

Schoenberg and His World, ed. Walter Frisch, Princeton: Princeton Univ. Press, 1999

Allen Shawn, *Arnold Schoenberg's Journey from Tone Poems to Kaleidoscopic Sound Colors,* Hillsdale NY: Pendragon Press, 2015

Brigitte Hamann, *Hitler's Vienna: A Portrait of the Tyrant as a Young Man,* London: Tauris Parke, 2010

Claire Beck Loos, *The Private Adolf Loos,* Los Angeles: DoppelHouse Press, 2011

Beverly Driver Eddy, Felix Salten: *Man of Many Faces,* Riverside CA: Ariadne Press, 2010

Alban Berg and His World, ed. Christopher Hailey, Princeton: Princeton Univ. Press, 2010

A Schoenberg Reader: Documents of a Life, ed. Joseph Auner, New Haven: Yale Univ. Press, 2003

Judith Cabaud, *Mathilde Wesendonck, ou, Le rêve d'Isolde,* Arles: Actes du Sud, 1990

Carl E. Schorske, *Fin de Siècle Vienna, Politics and Culture,* New York: Knopf, 1980

Georg Prochnik, *The Impossible Exile: Stefan Zweig at the End of the World,* New York: Other Press, 2014

Donald G. Daviau, *Der Mann von Übermorgen:* Hermann Bahr 1863–1934, Vienna: Österreichischer Bundesverlag, 1984

Stephen Beller, *Vienna and the Jews: A Cultural History 1867–1938,* Cambridge: Cambridge Unv. Press, 1995

Allan Janik, Stephen Toulin, *Wittgenstein's Vienna,* New York: Simon & Schuster, 1973

Frederic Spotts, *Hitler and The Power of Aesthetics,* London: Hutchinson, 2002

1

Here in New York I am often reminded of the popular song heard in the taverns of Vienna during my childhood:

The Christian, the Turk, the Heathen and the Jew
Have dwelt here in times old and new
Together in peace and free of strife
They are all entitled to live their own life.

Like every child in the empire, I knew the Kaiser's full title by heart: Franz Josef I, Emperor of Austria by the grace of God, King of Hungary and Bohemia, of Dalmatia, Croatia, Slovenia, Galicia, Lodomeria and Illyria; King of Jerusalem; Arch Duke of Austria; Grand Duke of Toscana and Krakow; Duke of Lothringia, of Salzburg, Steyer, Carinthia, Crain and Bukovina; Grand Duke of Transylvania; Margrave of Moravia; Duke of Upper and Lower Silesia, of Modena, Parma, Piacenza and Guastalla, of Auschwitz and Zator, of Teschen, Friaul, Ragusa and Zara; Princely Count of Hapsburg and Tyrol, of Kyburg, Göritz and Gradisca; Prince of Trient and Brixen; Margrave of Upper and Lower Lausitz and Istria; Count of Hohenembs, Feldkirch, Bregenz and Sonnenberg; Lord of Trieste, of Cattaro and Windic March; Great Duke of the Dukedom of Serbia.

In the early days of his reign, a law had been passed that all ethnic groups in the Austro-Hungarian Empire shared equal rights, and that each ethnic group had an inalienable right to preserve and cultivate its own nationality and language. In the first years of the century, more than half of

Vienna's population had not been born there, pouring in from all parts of the empire. Like today's New York, it became a magnet for refugees fleeing persecution, injustice and poverty, as well as others fleeing the law.

Although I am now called Otto Kallir, at that time my name was Nirenstein. My business was art; my gallery, the Neue Galerie, was situated in the centre of Vienna's old town, directly behind St. Stephen's cathedral, on the corner of Grünangergasse and Schulerstrasse, close to the house where Mozart had once lived. My passion was for the new art of the century. I believed in the future, in progress and the modern age – in science and in art.

One cold winter's day in early 1931, I was catching up with some routine paperwork in my first floor office. The gallery was quiet. Outside snow was piled high on the pavements and lay thick on the roofs of the buildings opposite, muffling the sound of the passing traffic and reflecting an eerie, pale light back into the room. As I stood up to warm myself in front of the blazing fire, there was a gentle tap on the half-open door.

'Herr Doktor?'

'Yes, Vita?'

'I don't wish to disturb you but there is a gentleman downstairs asking for you.'

'Did he say what he wants?'

'I'm sorry, Herr Doktor. His name is Alois Gerstl but he won't say any more – only that he would like to see you.'

'Don't worry, Vita, please show him up.'

My long-standing secretary Vita Maria Künstler retreated downstairs and quickly reappeared, accompanied by a solidly-built man in his early 50s. Alois Gerstl was carrying a small package. I went over to greet him.

'Thank you for seeing me, Doktor Nirenstein,' he began.

'It's no trouble, Herr Gerstl.'

I wasn't altogether surprised when he corrected me. 'It's Lieutenant Gerstl, in fact, although I left the military service a few years go.'

* * *

'How may I help you, Lieutenant Gerstl?'

'I was hoping you might be able to offer me some advice, as I know little about the art business.'

'I would be more than happy to try, Lieutenant. Please take a seat.'

'I'm much obliged, Herr Doktor', said Gerstl, 'I must apologise for turning up without notice'.

'Don't worry, Lieutenant. Tell me what I can do for you.'

I sat down again at my desk, while Alois Gerstl took the chair opposite me and began to explain. When his parents had passed away some years ago, he had been left a number of paintings, which had been kept in storage for over twenty years. He had rretired with only a small pension from a private bank, where he had more recently been employed. The storage costs didn't amount to a great deal but he now needed to be very careful about spending money unnecessarily, especially in the light of the country's current financial uncertainties. He was looking for an opinion on whether these paintings were worth keeping, or, if they had little value, whether it might be better to have them destroyed.

'If I might interrupt, Lieutenant Gerstl,' I said, 'can you tell me who these paintings are by?'

'My younger brother, Richard; he passed away in tragic circumstances in 1908 when only twenty five years of age. I collected a couple of small paintings the other day from the storage warehouse and took the liberty of bringing them to show you.'

When I displayed no objection, Alois Gerstl unwrapped the package he was carrying and produced two small canvasses. The paintings were covered in a fine film of dust. Both were landscapes with trees and orchards, immediately bringing to my mind the area around Grinzing on the northern outskirts of Vienna. I wet my finger and wiped it across a small part of the surface. The colours quickly came to life. I took a damp cloth and wiped the whole painting. It was immediately apparent that these were no traditional landscapes. Strikingly original, they were painted in a style almost unthinkable in the first years of the century. The afternoon sky had darkened and outside the window the first flakes of snow had started to fall over the cold, grey city once more. Alois Gerstl accepted my offer of a cognac.

'Tell me more about your brother, Lieutenant Gerstl,' I prompted him. While I went over to the cabinet to pour two small glasses, he began to relate something of his family history.

His father Emil was a Jew, born in Hungary. After moving to Vienna, he had met his mother Maria, who was a Catholic. Emil Gerstl had made his money as an investor in the stock market, before becoming a partner in the family firm of wool merchants. Alois and his older brother August were born out of wedlock but, shortly before his second brother Richard was born, in 1883, his mother converted to Judaism, and they were married in a Jewish ceremony. Richard, however, was baptised a Catholic, as his mother had quickly turned her back on her new religion.

They had lived at numerous addresses in Alsergrund. At that time the newly-built apartments there were popular with the growing number of assimilated Jewish middle class professionals, many of whom aspired to move out of the traditional Jewish district of Leopoldstadt. Eventually they had settled in an apartment in the Nussdorferstrasse, near the Liechtenstein Park. With his brothers, Alois attended primary school in the Bartensteingasse, behind the Parliament building, before Richard was sent to the Maria Treu Church School. That had proved something of a disaster. He soon came into conflict with the Piarist Fathers' strict authoritarian regime, and he was moved again to a private school in the Buchfeldgasse.

'Prost!' I said, raising my glass.

'Prost!' Lieutenant Gerstl reciprocated, visibly relaxing somewhat and continuing with his story. Their mother had always encouraged Richard in his artistic interests and she managed to persuade his more reluctant father to send him for private drawing lessons with Otto Frey, a student at the Academy. Frey quickly recognised some precocious talent in Richard and advised preparing him for the entrance examination at the Academy of Fine Art. After a summer course at the Aula Drawing School,

Richard was accepted for the Academy's General Painting Class under Professor Griepenkerl. That was in the autumn of 1898 when Richard had only just turned fifteen.

'If you don't mind me asking, were you and Richard close?' I enquired.

'Even as a boy,' Alois Gerstl replied, 'Richard seemed to enjoy his own company but we got on well enough. It was less so with Richard and my elder brother. But once I started my army career, I was often stationed away from home, so I saw less of Richard. At the Academy he had become acquainted with a fellow student, Viktor Hammer, who could tell you much more about Richard's time there. When I came back on leave, I would sometimes spend time with them both. Although I didn't know all the details, I soon discovered that Richard's ideas and personality had clashed quite dramatically with Griepenkerl's. As a result, Richard broke off his official studies in his second year.'

Nevertheless, with his mother's support, Richard persuaded his father to keep funding him and continued more intensely with his painting. He rented a private studio in a villa on the Hohe Warte, where, as well as painting, he educated himself more widely, particularly in languages and music. He rarely missed any concert or performance of note in Vienna and soon became well acquainted with the radical circle of composers, musicians and writers centred on Arnold Schönberg and Alexander von Zemlinsky. In fact, Richard painted portraits of several members of the group. Alois had been told that my gallery had exhibited some of Schoenberg's paintings and as a consequence, decided to approach me.

'Did your brother ever exhibit or sell any of these paintings?' I asked.

'Not as far as I am aware. I think there was an occasional commissioned portrait but painted more as a favour. Almost all his paintings seem to be of people he knew well, including my mother and me. Even father eventually agreed to be painted in our apartment.' There were also quite a few more landscapes, which he had painted locally in and around Vienna and on the shores of the Traunsee in the Salzkammergut, where he spent his last two summers at the invitation of the Schönbergs.

'Forgive me, Lieutenant Gerstl, have I missed something?', I asked. What I still don't understand is why his paintings were never exhibited and have been left abandoned in a warehouse for so many years.'

Alois Gerstl considered his reply for a short time, as if making a decision. He took a sip of cognac, before hesitatingly and somewhat reluctantly taking up his story again.

'Herr Doktor, it's still a delicate matter but I will tell you everything I know. Something of a scandal surrounded my brother's death, which was officially attributed to mental instability. On the night of the 4th of November 1908, Richard stabbed himself in the chest with a knife and hung himself in front of the mirror at his studio in the Liechtensteinstrasse, after apparently attempting to burn some of his drawings, letters and personal effects.'

I was deeply shocked and more than a little embarrassed. 'My sincere apologies, Lieutenant Gerstl, I really had no idea. I don't know what to say.'

'There is no need to be sorry, Herr Doktor. There is no way you could have known and it was all a long time ago. The family decided to keep the details as quiet as possible.' They had salvaged everything that had not been destroyed, before clearing all the paintings from the studio and placing them into storage at the warehouse of Rosin & Knauer, where they had remained for the past twenty three years.

'Well, Lieutenant Gerstl,' I replied, 'if you are agreeable, I think it's more than time that your brother's paintings saw the light of day again.'

2

A few days later, accompanied by Alois Gerstl, I went to the warehouse of Rosin and Knauer in Alsergrund. It was immediately obvious that it would be almost impossible to view the paintings properly there, so I arranged for the paintings to be collected from the warehouse and delivered to the gallery. Together with Gerstl, Vita Künstler and my general assistant Carl Fügl, we gradually opened up the large wooden cases into which the paintings had been packed. The canvasses had been taken off their stretchers, then rolled or crudely folded for over twenty years. Some paintings were torn and others had even been cut into pieces. Though they were all covered in a thick grey dust, it was immediately clear that there was some considerable damage to the surface of the paintings.

We unpacked the paintings slowly, one by one; the smaller ones first. These were mostly more landscapes, presumably as his brother had said, of the lakes and mountains of the Salzkammergut. They were painted in an extreme expressionist style but years, apparently, before that term had been invented. A few others were recognisable as Viennese subjects: the vineyards around Grinzing and Nussdorf on the outskirts of the city; a view of buildings across the Danube canal; a street scene, identified by his brother as the view from the window of the family apartment in the Nussdorferstrasse.

However, the majority of the paintings, which numbered over fifty in total, were of people. Though not conventional portraits in any sense of the word, some subjects his brother and I could instantly identify: his elderly father sat by his desk in his study; Alois himself standing upright in his officer's uniform; Arnold Schönberg's great friend and brother-in-law Alexander von Zemlinsky in his white suit standing by a lakeshore; I also recognised a younger Ernst Diez, an art historian, an acquaintance of mine, who was a cousin of composer Anton Webern. More remarkable still were a number of haunting öportraits. They included a life-size painting of the artist standing naked at his easel against a swirling, violet-blue background, as well a particularly disturbing small canvas, which depicted him shaven-headed, lit by a lamp or candle below him in the darkness of his studio, grinning scornfully back at the viewer. Even more shocking were two large group portraits, one recognisably of the Schönberg family, the other a larger group portrait, both vividly-coloured and painted in a maelstrom of violent brush marks.

As I looked on in silent astonishment, I resolved immediately to do everything I could to rescue this forgotten artist's name from oblivion, even though it was clear that a great deal of time, effort and money would be required to restore the paintings to a condition in which they could be exhibited. Before leaving, Alois Gerstl handed me a thick envelope. This, he said, contained all his brother's surviving personal effects saved from the fire in the studio. Apart from the few enclosed letters he had received concerning his brother after his death, he had neither read nor opened any of them.

Liechtensteinstrasse 68/70
Vienna IX

November 6th 1908

Dear Herr Gerstl,

I am sincerely grateful to you for your message. I will not attend the funeral, as it would be too distressing for your parents to see me. Poor Richard doesn't know anything any longer. May I ask you to let me know the number of Richard's grave as soon as you can? I hope I will see you again.

With my best regards,
Mathilde Schönberg

Liechtensteinstrasse 68/70
Vienna IX

November 8th 1908

Dear Herr Gerstl,

My deepest thanks for all the trouble you have taken. I would have much preferred to speak to you in person but I am feeling so wretched and depressed because of the terrible events that it wasn't really possible. I still hope we can speak once everything has settled down. In case you discover anything in Richard's studio which you believe may belong to me, may I ask you to destroy it? Please do not send me anything, as it is all so terribly painful for me and it would only remind me of this tragic disaster. Please believe me, out of the two of us, Richard has taken the easiest way. To have to live in such circumstances is extremely hard.

Take care, and as I said before, I hope I haven't spoken to you for the last time.

Yours,
Mathilde Schönberg

Liechtensteinstrasse 68/70
Vienna IX

November 9th 1908

Dear Sir,

I do not know if I have the right to ask you a favour; but I do believe that, as the innocent party in this affair, who has suffered and continues to suffer, you will not deny me this.

I am afraid that when the true cause of your poor brother's death is discovered, the newspapers, in view of my standing, will make the matter a public sensation and, to a greater or lesser extent, will turn me though blameless into a laughing stock. You will surely not want this to happen, and neither would your brother! Even if I myself managed to survive it! My God, there have been so many things lately that I have had to overcome, this would just be yet another! But for the sake of my wife, you ought to prevent this happening, and I believe this is what your brother would have wanted too!

Perhaps it is possible that it could all be explained as a grievance about a lack of success. There is no benefit to you in my discomfort; it is merely a question of offering a reason which will avoid sensation. I very much hope that you will afford me this consideration, and I thank you in advance.

Respectfully,
Arnold Schönberg

3

Before the art world, my first love had been aviation. At just fifteen years of age, I had written a History of Aeronautics, recording man's early attempts at flight: from the Montgolfier brothers' hot-air balloons in the latter part of the eighteenth century through to Orville and Wilbur Wright's pioneering experiments. The book was published by my uncle, a lithographer, with whose firm, H. Engels and Son, I served a short apprenticeship. Aviation, I enthusiastically predicted, would soon exceed all expectations and become the safest and fastest means of transport in the world, even though at that time, in 1909, no aircraft had yet flown over water or carried any person aloft for more than a few minutes. While I loved the flights I later made as an observer over Italy, serving as a junior officer in the Great War and fighting on both the Italian and Russian fronts, my own flying aspirations were cut short, due to my wife's concern for my safety.

Nevertheless, I continued to pursue my passion obsessively as an historian and collector, amassing a vast horde of aeronautical memorabilia: books, stamps, medals and autographs, as well as significant historical documents, including a compendium of propaganda leaflets with rare items heralding the Russian Revolution, jointly signed by Lenin and Trotsky, and others by the Italian nationalist Gabriele D'Annunzio, which for me carried a particular nostalgia.

Poet and literary celebrity, D'Annunzio had flown with Wilbur Wright in 1908 and volunteered in the war as a fighter pilot, losing an eye in a flying accident. While Italian morale was still reeling from the rout by the Austro-Hungarian troops at the Battle of Caporetto, D'Annunzio instigated a daring raid on the harbour at Bakar in February 1918, helping to restore some degree of Italian national pride. In August that same year, as commander of the 87th fighter squadron *La Serenissima*, it was D'Annunzio who planned the Flight over Vienna, one of the most extraordinary feats of the war. As a young man, I was fortunate to see the eleven planes, led by D'Annunzio himself in a round trip of over 1200 kilometres, which dropped thousands of propaganda leaflets over the city. The biplane he flew that day now hangs suspended in the auditorium of Il Vittoriale, his villa at Gardone Riviera on the shores of Lake Garda, which now houses his idiosyncratic collection of bizarre objects.

After the war, the growing tide of anti-Semitism, which by then had permeated many professions in Vienna, frustrated my hopes of becoming an engineer. The art world, fortunately, had no such barriers. So, instead, in 1919, I joined the prestigious Viennese Fine Art gallery and publishers, Würthle and Sons, owned by Lea Bondi Jaray, whose husband Sandor, a successful sculptor, was part of the wealthy Jaray family, Imperial furniture makers. I was soon delegated responsibility for the Verlag Neuer Graphik, Würthle's publishing arm, specialising in original art prints and deluxe limited edition books. As I had received a basic grounding in painting and drawing, and for a time dreamt of becoming an artist, the opportunity to combine dealing in art with the more traditional Jewish profession of publishing greatly appealed to me. My father, a lawyer, who had lost most of his assets in the economic upheaval following the collapse of the empire, viewed it as a slightly sordid commercial activity however, a regression to the traditional Jewish role of shopkeeper: 'behind the counter' was his contemptuous phrase.

My first publication was a portfolio of ten original lithographs by my former art teacher, Johannes Itten. Itten had set up the private art school in Vienna in 1916, where I was briefly a student while home on army sick leave, recovering from pleurisy. It was there that he had begun to develop the revolutionary teaching methods which he was later to introduce to the Bauhaus school in Weimar. The set of lithographs was included in an exhibition of Itten's paintings in the Kärntnerstrasse, organised by the 'Freie Bewegung' Artists' Association. This was run by probably the most influential single figure in Viennese art circles, the architect, Adolf Loos, who also introduced me to many other well-known artists and writers.

4

In 1921, Lea Bondi Jaray decided to sell Gallery Würthle's Verlag Neuer Graphik to the banker Richard Kola, who was building a vast publishing empire, and at the time was considered to be the richest man in Austria. With his financial backing, I continued an ambitious series of publications over the next two years: lavishly-bound editions containing original graphics by modern Austrian artists, including, amongst others, Julius Zimpel, Oskar Laske, Alfred Kubin, Gustav Klimt and Egon Schiele. But, as fast as it had prospered, Kola's empire swiftly declined into bankruptcy. When Kola's eponymous Rikola Verlag finally collapsed, I decided it was time to set up my own independent business.

I found vacant premises on the corner of the Grünangergasse in the heart of the old city, a convenient walking distance from my apartment in the Mahlergasse. The tall, narrow building, with its warren of rooms behind an elegant modern Art Nouveau facade, easily lent itself to both gallery space and publishing offices. Initially, the gallery comprised just three exhibition rooms with a couple of rooms for offices, but as the years went on expanded to occupy the whole building with fifteen rooms in total. I employed a young man, Carl Fügl, as my general helper, and, a short while later, a secretary, Dr. Vita Maria Künstler, who had studied Art History at the University of Vienna. While still a student, she had been a regular at my gallery's exhibition openings. When I asked her what she intended to do after graduation, Vita had bluntly said 'look for a job!' 'Come and work as my secretary,' I immediately replied and she quickly became my trusted and indispensable assistant.

During the war, I had made the acquaintance of the journalist, Max Roden, a major collector of modern Austrian art. On his advice, I contacted the controversial artist, Egon Schiele, with a view to buying some of his work as an investment, but it came to nothing at the time due to my father's disapproval. Nevertheless, my fascination with Schiele had only increased with the passing of the years. The opening exhibition in the Neue Galerie in the late autumn of 1923 was dedicated entirely to his paintings, watercolours and drawings although, disappointingly, it found few ready buyers. The public interest in Schiele had waned since his premature death from the Spanish flu epidemic, which had swept through Europe at the end of the war. I quickly learned that, if the gallery was to survive, I would need to be more pragmatic and support my own interests with more profitable dealing in traditional nineteenth century painters, better suited to the conservative tastes of the rising Viennese middle-classes. Through Loos' fellow habitué from the Café Central, the writer Hugo von Hofmannsthal, I had also met Fanny von Löwenstein, a close friend of the famous writer's daughter. Fanny and I were married soon afterwards, but I now needed to earn enough money to support a family.

In conjunction with the Austrian Artists' Society, the Hagenbund, I arranged regular loan exhibitions of the latest developments in modern European art: Russian painters including Chagall, Kandinsky and El Lissitzky; the Norwegian, Edvard Munch; a Lovis Corinth memorial exhibition, as well as his fellow German Expressionist, Max Beckmann; French Impressionists and Post-Impressionists, including Degas, Renoir, Manet and Cézanne; sculptures by Rodin, Gauguin and Picasso; and, above all, a two-part show of works by Vincent van Gogh. These were predominantly non-selling exhibitions but they helped me build more interest in the Viennese moderns I loved, such as Klimt and Kokoschka, as well as Schiele of course, all of whom could now be seen in the wider context of their European peers.

During the second half of the twenties, as the economy boomed, the gallery business thrived but the foreign investment which had flowed into

Austria and Central Europe proved short-lived. Much of the money had stemmed from the United States, where, following 'Black Tuesday' and the Wall Street Crash in October 1929, foreign loans were quickly recalled. The repercussions were soon felt throughout Europe and, in September 1930, there was a run on the Reichsbank, which lost one million Reichsmarks in less than a month. Germany immediately announced it could no longer continue its enormous reparation payments. The panic quickly spread to Austria, throwing the government into crisis when it was forced to come to the rescue of its largest bank, the Rothschilds-owned Creditanstalt.

As money dried up, the art market suffered dramatically. I decided to stage exhibitions of lower-priced paintings and diversify into other more affordable areas of collecting: handcrafts and folk art from Poland and Hungary; the new art of photography; Russian icons; rare stamps; original manuscripts by Johann Strauss; historical documents from the Great War; even an exhibition of my own collection of aeronautical memorabilia. In the evenings, I hired out the gallery to the theatrical director Carl Heinz Roth for drama classes, and with the help of the well-known actor and comedian Fritz Grünbaum, former master of ceremonies at the Cabaret Hölle, I worked as a photographer for the theatrical press. Grünbaum had long been one of my best clients, amassing a large and significant collection of works by Schiele, in particular. I now hoped that the discovery of Richard Gerstl's lost paintings might also provide me with a unique opportunity to boost business.

Neue Galerie
Grünangergasse 1
Vienna I

To:
Herrn Alois Gerstl
Schönburgstrasse 32
Vienna IV

28th May 1931

Dear Lieutenant Gerstl,

I hereby confirm our verbal agreement as follows: I agree to purchase from you the thirty six paintings in my possession by your brother Richard Gerstl (who passed away in 1908) for the total sum of 1400 Austrian schillings. On the conclusion of this agreement you will receive an immediate payment of seven hundred schillings. The remaining seven hundred schillings will be paid to you in monthly payments of one hundred schillings, starting on 1st July 1931 and ending on 31st December 1931. If I should wish to purchase any further paintings or the other drawings still in your possession, I will pay you a further one hundred schillings deposit immediately.

All reproduction rights hereby pass to me, not only for the paintings I have purchased but for your brother's complete works. A number of paintings, which are still in storage at Roisin and Knauer, remain in your ownership. If the planned exhibition in the autumn proves a financial success, I confirm my intention to purchase the remaining paintings from you for a price still to be negotiated or, if we cannot reach an agreement on terms, then I will undertake to sell any work individually on your behalf at a 10% commission rate. You have agreed to place at my disposal any other relevant documentation about your brother, which is in your possession or is discovered at a later date, as well as support me when the opportunity arises in any further research for the purpose of reconstructing a fuller picture of your brother's career.

In the meantime, I would be grateful if you would indicate your agreement by signing the enclosed copy of the agreement.

With my regards,

Yours sincerely,
Doktor Otto Nirenstein

5

Standing in front of the entwined figures of Gustav Klimt's 'The Kiss', Viktor Hammer recalled seeing the painting when it was first exhibited.

'Gerstl and I visited the Kunstschau exhibition together in June 1908. The exhibition took place on empty land near the Stadtpark where the Konzerthaus now stands,' said Hammer. 'It was conceived by Klimt and some of his fellow Secessionist artists, architects and designers to celebrate the Kaiser's Golden Jubilee. In only a few months, they created over fifty exhibition rooms, as well as courtyards, gardens, a café and an outdoor stage.'

'Yes, I was still quite young but I do remember it', I replied. 'Didn't they borrow the famous inscription from the facade of the Secession building?'

'That's right – with its motto 'To the age its art; to art its freedom'. They placed it at the entrance to the main exhibition pavilion. The Kaiser's official procession was intended to highlight the empire's ethnic diversity and long tradition, while the Kunstschau, Klimt proclaimed in his opening speech, was a celebration of artistic freedom in Austria by artists who had no allegiance to any group or collective.'

'What was Gerstl's attitude?' I asked.

'Gerstl had little time for either the official parade or the unofficial exhibition. And he reserved his particular derision for the centrepiece of the exhibition, the two rooms devoted entirely to Klimt's paintings. In his opinion, Klimt was only interested in decorating the drawing rooms of the affluent Jewish bourgeoisie, filling them with his canvasses gleaming in gold and silver.'

I had arranged to meet Richard Gerstl's former student friend at the recently opened Moderne Galerie in the Orangery of the Belvedere Palace. Hammer was now known as a fine draughtsman and illustrator, as well as a printer of small, fine editions with a special interest in typography. Self-contained and articulate, he chose his words carefully and had the slightly pedantic air of an academic professor, exuding a confident and ingrained knowledge of his subject. Now approaching fifty, he still appeared physically youthful, a thick head of hair carefully brushed back from a high forehead, below which he wore large round spectacles.

On a bright, early spring morning, we walked the short distance across the Belvedere's formal gardens to the smaller and more private Schweizergarten nearby, where we sat at a table in the small café-restaurant and ordered coffee. The seclusion of the surrounding streams, ponds and rose garden made it an ideal place for conversation, as Viktor Hammer told me about his early years.

'I was brought up in Vienna's inner city. In fact, we lived for a number of years in the Schönlaterngasse, around the corner from where your gallery now is, Herr Doktor. Even as a boy, I was more interested in drawing than schoolwork. At sixteen, I became a student at the Academy of Fine Arts and remained there for ten years. That was how I first encountered Richard Gerstl, when we both enrolled under Professor Christian Griepenkerl in the winter semester of 1898.'

'Wasn't Griepenkerl originally the student of Carl Rahl?' I asked.

'That's right,' Hammer replied, 'they both specialised in allegory and history painting. Rahl, of course, is best known for The Triumph of Harmony, his design for the Staatsoper curtain for tragic opera. Griepenkerl assisted him on frescoes in many of Vienna's civic buildings, and, after Rahl died, he succeeded him as Vienna's leading decorative painter; his frescoes and ceiling paintings still adorn many of the public buildings along the Ringstrasse, including the Opera House, the Academy of Fine Arts and the Parliament. Essentially, he was a died-in-the-wool conservative and traditionalist, who considered the explosion of new ideas in painting as a fashionable aberration. Even though I was also drawn towards craftsmanship in art, I soon realised that Griepenkerl was firmly locked into 19th century ideas. That impressed Gerstl even less.'

'What kind of character was Gerstl in those days?'

'Generally quiet and reserved, with rather a shy nature. Slightly insecure. I don't quite know how to explain it. He often seemed restless, rather discontent in himself. He never mixed much with the rest of the students and was quite solitary, seemingly happy in his own company. However he held very firm opinions, particularly on art, and quickly became passionate, even fiery, if challenged. Despite that he could be kind and generous. Apart from Waldemar Unger, the son of family friends and a law student at the University, I suppose I was the only fellow student who could be regarded as Gerstl's friend. I must admit, in spite of the number of years which have passed, Herr Doktor, I never thought I had heard the last of Richard Gerstl.'

'Although we soon became friends, our approach to painting could not have been more different. I aspired to become a portrait artist and painted in a realistic style, modeled on the Old Masters, while Gerstl was always interested in painting in a modern way, contrary to Griepenkerl's insistence on traditional academic techniques. Despite that, he admired Rembrandt and Velázquez, in particular, and would often sit copying paintings in the Kunsthistorisches Museum. One day, when he was asked if he had permission to be there, he snapped back, 'What has it got to do with you?', only to discover it was actually the Museum Director. But he became obsessive about the new developments in French painting, which the regular Secessionist exhibitions introduced to Vienna.'

I was already well acquainted with the history of the Secessionist movement. When Klimt and Carl Moll, Alma Mahler's stepfather, dramatically resigned from the Association of Viennese Artists, they had taken with them a number of other members to form the Secession. The Secessionists demanded the right of free artistic expression. Their main supporter, the critic Hermann Bahr, had voiced their feelings: 'The Artists'

Association is just a market, a bazaar; let the merchants there offer their wares. Inevitably, some friends of the arts will be forced to unite and hire a few well-lit venues in the city to show the Viennese what is happening in European art.'

They soon managed a great deal better than that. Financed by industrialist Karl Wittgenstein and designed by architect Joseph Olbrich, a new temple to the arts, complete with gilded dome, was erected on the Karlsplatz, opposite the baroque Karlskirche. The 'gilded cabbage', as it quickly became known, opened in 1898, the same year, in fact, as Hammer and Gerstl enrolled at the Academy. The first exhibition attracted well over fifty thousand visitors.

'We visited each Secessionist exhibition religiously,' Hammer went on. 'It was there at the second exhibition when we first saw the Pointillist paintings of Belgian artist, Theo van Rysselberghe, which made a huge impression on Gerstl, particularly his blazing colours, which were of such a joy and intensity that you felt as if you had stepped into the sun itself. No doubt, Herr Doktor, you're aware of the scandal over Klimt's large Philosophy panel in the 1900 exhibition, which he was commissioned to paint for the great hall of the University?' Hammer asked.

'Yes, of course. I know there was an enormous storm of protest with the public and the press and it even caused a famous row in the parliament. What was Gerstl's reaction?'

'He sided with Karl Kraus, who sarcastically asked in his popular satirical magazine *Die Fackel* whether anyone was really interested in how Klimt imagined Philosophy,' Hammer replied. 'And he was just as contemptuous of what he saw as Klimt's ornate and stylised symbolism. From that time on, in fact, Gerstl never had a good word to say about Klimt – although he never missed an opportunity of seeing his latest work.'

'Gerstl's brother has told me that he also ran into some difficulties at the Academy.'

'Yes, that's right. Rather predictably, Gerstl's increasing fascination with the radical new movements in painting wasn't shared by Professor

Griepenkerl, even though he consistently marked his work as 'satisfactory' in his end-of-term reports with praise for his application and conduct. As a result of his growing frustration with the Academy's insistence on tradition, Gerstl persuaded his father to pay for him to accompany me to the summer painting school at Nagybánya, which Simon Hollósy had set up in his native Hungary as the summer retreat from the painting school he ran in Munich. It attracted students from all over Europe, concentrating on a much more naturalistic approach, painting landscapes outdoors in a style influenced by the artists of the French Barbizon School.'

'On our return to the Academy, the influence of his time in Nagybánya soon began to appear in Gerstl's paintings. Unsurprisingly, it found little favour with Griepenkerl, who told him bluntly one day – please excuse my language Herr Doktor – 'The way you paint, I can piss in the snow.' Once he came back from his second summer in Nagybánya in 1901, Gerstl refused to return to the Academy for the winter term and rented a studio in the Therese-Krones-Haus in Heiligenstadt.'

'Aside from a single term in 1904, Gerstl didn't go back to the Academy for another five years. We remained good friends however and met frequently in the city or on the Hohe Warte, when we would often go walking in the surrounding countryside. Gerstl had continued his own independent studies and considerably broadened his education, reading extensively in philosophy and psychology. He closely followed the latest developments in literature and, even more so, in music, as well as teaching himself several foreign languages that had enabled him to study, among other things, scientific writings on colour theory. I always looked forward to our walks when Gerstl would talk to me enthusiastically about his latest interests.'

6

Hammer recalled that on one occasion Gerstl spoke a great about the Leipzig neurologist Paul Julius Möbius, whose book *On the Physiological Basis of Feeblemindedness in Women* had recently caused something of a stir. Möbius claimed that women's tendency towards narrower heads was a sign of inferiority. Gerstl jokingly said he had measured his own and discovered it was seventy one centimetres wide. He had also read Möbius' psychological studies on great figures in European culture, such as Goethe, Schumann and Nietzsche, termed 'pathographies', which investigated the connections between creative genius and pathological conditions. Möbius' research into the causes of mental dysfunction and the psychotherapeutic treatment of hysteria had also been closely studied by the controversial Viennese doctor Sigmund Freud. Gerstl's family had lived for a short time directly opposite his treatment rooms and apartment in the Berggasse. Published in 1899 in only six hundred copies, Freud's *Interpretation of Dreams* had not attracted many initial readers but Gerstl was one of them. He was fascinated, said Hammer, by Freud's observation that while the waking mind thinks through language, in dreams the mind creates hallucinations, replacing words with images. This, Gerstl believed, would instigate a radical change in the subject matter of painting.

What also intrigued Gerstl, Hammer went on, was how art could foreshadow scientific and medical discoveries. In relation to Freud's ideas, he cited Wedekind's drama *Spring Awakening*, where the dawning of children's sexual curiosity is sacrificed to fear and social control, masquerading as morality. His indictment of a hypocritical educational system clearly struck a chord with Gerstl, said Hammer. The play ended in the accidental death of one main character and the suicide of the other. Gerstl told Hammer that he had attended a private performance at the tiny Trianon Theatre of another work by Wedekind, *Pandora's Box*, arranged by Kraus, in which the author himself played the part of Jack the Ripper. Following its premiere in Nürnberg, both Wedekind and his publisher had been charged with obscenity, and the play was immediately banned by the German authorities. Gerstl wryly remarked that its themes of death, suicide and sexual desire, oblivious to moral or social constraints, had found its natural home in Vienna.

However, the most influential book for Gerstl at that time, Hammer revealed, was written by a fellow Viennese student. Both Freud and Möbius had complained that the book which had become the talk of Viennese intellectual circles, *Sex and Character* by the young University philosophy graduate, Otto Weininger, had stolen their ideas. Son of a Jewish goldsmith, who was also an avid admirer of Wagner, Weininger was a brilliant student with a special talent for languages. At the same time as Hammer and Gerstl entered the Academy in the autumn of 1898, the 18-year-old Weininger enrolled in the Philosophical Faculty at Vienna University, much against his father's wishes. He was a passionate debater, often upsetting his tutors, and he soon joined the university's Philosophical Society, which held weekly lectures by leading figures in their field on a wide range of subjects from Darwinism and the natural sciences to art and music.

Increasingly dissatisfied and frustrated with scientific research, Weininger's restless nature took him on a long, solitary journey into psychology, literature and philosophy. Soon after finishing his doctoral thesis, in which he argued that ethics was the only subject that mattered, he converted to Protestantism, the religion of his hero Immanuel Kant. The conversion from Judaism to Christianity, from the body to morality, was his solution to overcoming the Jewish self; the choice, he said, was between business and culture, woman and man, the race and the individual, unworthiness and worth, the sensual and the spiritual life, between nothingness and the God-like. Christ was the absolute example of overcoming the Jewish self; a man possessed by a great idea, who had abandoned human and social ties.

According to Weininger, the modern age was not only the most Jewish but also the most effeminate of all ages; an age of the most credulous anarchism, without any appreciation of the state or law; an age of the shallowest of all imaginable interpretations of history, of Capitalism and Marxism; an age in which everything was defined by economics and technology. It also had the distinction of being the first age not only to have affirmed and worshipped sexual intercourse but to have practically made it a duty, not as a way of achieving oblivion, as the Romans and Greeks had done in their bacchanals, but in order to give its own dreary existence some meaning. All individuals, he believed, divided into those who loved themselves and those who hated themselves. He began to see the battle between good and evil, guilt and salvation, within himself.

Weininger's inner struggles resulted in a growing emotional crisis and severe depression. 'I have the chill of the grave in me', he said, feeling incapable of living up to his own ideas and strict moral code. Returning to Vienna from a trip to Italy in September 1903, he rented rooms in a former monastery behind the Votivkirche in the Schwarzspanierstrasse, where Beethoven had lived his final days. A few days later in early October, he shot himself through the heart and died in hospital the same day, aged twenty three. It was claimed that during his funeral a partial eclipse took place, which ended at precisely the same moment as his body was lowered into the grave. On his gravestone in the Matzleinsdorf Protestant Cemetery his father wrote his epitaph:

This stone closes the resting place of a young man
Whose mind never found peace on this earth
And after offering us the revelations of his mind and soul
He could no longer bear to be among the living.

He searched for the place of death of one of the greatest spirits
Who had dwelled in the house in Schwarzspanierstrasse
And put an end to his mortal existence.

The manner and place of his death, as well as his reputation as an eccentric genius, became something of a cause célèbre in the Viennese press. Worshipped by some, and attacked by others, *Sex and Character* quickly became a best-seller, translated into numerous languages. The publishers claimed that no book in the history of science had been so popular.

Gerstl, said Hammer, identified with Weininger, just three years his senior, as a fellow outsider, who shared a similar background. He took Hammer to visit the house in the Schwarzspanierstrasse, where Weininger had died, just a five minute walk from Gerstl's home. Weininger's rejection of decadent values and quest for a solution to the meaninglessness of modern life made him an intellectual hero not only for Gerstl but for a generation which empathised with his final verdict on the human condition, 'The human being is alone in the universe, in eternal monstrous solitude.'

7

'On our way back from Grinzing one day,' Hammer continued, 'Gerstl surprised me by asking if I would be interested to visit his studio. He said he had recently finished a self-portrait influenced by Weininger's ideas, and, in particular, his view of Christ as the ultimate example of transcendence through self-sacrifice. His isolated studio was situated close by on the Hohe Warte on the first floor of a large villa. I hadn't seen any of Gerstl's paintings since he had left the Academy and I was astounded by what he showed me. Propped up in the corner of the large Wintergarten studio next to the full length window, Gerstl's self-portrait was life-size; the bottom edge of the canvas cutting off the totally symmetrical figure just below the knees, giving the impression that it was emerging out of the picture towards me. Set against a deep turquoise background, painted with a vigorous swirl of brushstrokes, Gerstl's image was surrounded by a glowing halo of paler blue-green light. His slender figure was naked to the waist, wearing only a white loin cloth, which clearly recalled the baptised or newly-resurrected Christ. The artist's gaze was penetrating and transfixing. It was unlike any other painting I had ever seen, creating an eerie, other-worldly impression.'

'Yes, I understand exactly what you mean. That painting is among those I acquired from his brother. It's a very strange and haunting work. Were there any other paintings in his studio?' I asked.

'There was just one other, as I recall: a vast double portrait still in its early stages. Gerstl said the sitters were Pauline and Karoline Fey, daughters of his father's friend, a state insurance official, who lived in a villa nearby in Döbling. To be frank, Herr Doktor, at that time I didn't really understand his paintings or know what to say about them, so instead I told him how fortunate he was to have such a large space of his own to work in. To my great surprise, Gerstl generously replied that I would be welcome to share it with him. As I was then obliged to paint either at the Academy or in a small room at home, I gratefully took him up on his offer. Once I moved in, we thought it would be interesting to take turns to paint self-portraits, using the large mirror in the studio. This time, Gerstl stood, soberly dressed, holding his palette and brushes, his earlier self-portrait visible in the background.'

Sharing Gerstl's studio also gave Hammer the opportunity to observe the progress of his portrait of the sisters at first hand during the following winter months. By Easter, the painting was virtually complete. On an even larger scale than his self-portrait, the two sisters sat side by side on a divan, pressed so tightly together there was no visible space between them. Like the self-portrait, they faced the viewer directly with piercing but expressionless dark eyes; unlike the self-portrait, the painting was executed in a virtually monochromatic palette, the sisters wearing identical white shawls over diaphanous ball gowns, which spread out to fill most of the lower half of the painting. Despite being painted in their home, there was no obviously identifiable location; the background was a mass of black and ochre brushstrokes, still visible behind the transparency of the dresses, streaking its shades of white with greys and yellows.

'That is another painting which has been kept in storage for all these years although it has suffered considerable damage,' I replied. 'I'm grateful for that information. We had been unable to identify the sitters until now. Certainly anything less like a conventional society portrait would be difficult to imagine.'

'Exactly, Herr Doktor.' Hammer replied. 'I thought I could recognise some influence of the Norwegian artist, Edvard Munch, whose controversial paintings, at the invitation of the Secessionist President, Alfred Roller, had filled an entire room in the previous year's exhibition. Although

I never heard Gerstl talk much about him, I could see more than an echo of Munch.'

'I understand what you are saying. It certainly has Munch's typical expressionless faces and his vigorous use of paint. But, on the other hand, Gerstl's painting seems to avoid any traces of the Norwegian's symbolism, which has the effect of making it even more disturbing and impenetrable.'

Hammer then explained how he had decided to leave Griepenkerl's classes at the Academy in order to enroll in Heinrich Lefler's more advanced Special School, whose purpose was to prepare students to become full-time professional artists. Lefler had been a founding member of the Hagenbund Artists' Association, working as chief stage designer under Mahler at the Court Opera. He became Professor at the Academy in 1903, at the same time continuing his interest in stage and costume design at the Burgtheater, which brought him into regular contact with Vienna's literary circles. Even though he had studied under Griepenkerl and was himself a more traditional artist, as a result of his musical and literary connections, Lefler had a more open-minded attitude towards the new movements in modern painting. Hammer persuaded Gerstl to consider returning to the Academy to resume his studies in Lefler's classes and arranged for him to visit Gerstl in his studio. Astonished by the monumental portrait of the Fey sisters, not only did Lefler invite Gerstl to join his Special School class, he also agreed to Gerstl's request for a private studio space. Consequently, in the summer semester of 1906, Gerstl returned to the Academy on the Schillerplatz.

Lefler's connection with Mahler earned him Gerstl's immediate respect, said Hammer, and gave them a common interest. During his years away from the Academy, Gerstl had become such an ardent enthusiast of modern music that he had even considered a career as a music critic. He rarely missed any concert or opera of significance and had got to know a number of musicians and composers, including violinist and conductor Arnold Rose, who was married to Mahler's sister. One day in front of the Parliament building, Gerstl told Hammer, he had encountered Mahler by chance and introduced himself. He asked if the Hofoper Director would be willing to sit for a portrait but Mahler had politely declined, excusing himself on grounds of lack of time.

8

'Unfortunately I will be leaving Vienna in a few days' time, Herr Doktor,' Hammer explained. 'I must return to London for an exhibition of my paintings. So, if you still have time, there is somewhere I thought I would show you. It's not very far.'

'I am in no rush, Herr Hammer,' I replied. 'I would be very curious.'

We retraced our path through the perfectly-manicured gardens of the Belvedere Palace with the city spread out in front of us, its skyline dominated by the Gothic spire of St. Stephen's Cathedral. Hammer resumed his story as we walked.

Just after he had returned to the Academy in the spring of 1906, Gerstl attended a performance at the Hofoper of Wagner's *Tristan und Isolde* conducted by Mahler. Recognising Schönberg and Zemlinsky there, he approached them to ask if they would be willing to sit for portraits. Both composers were well acquainted with Professor Lefler, and Schönberg contacted him to find out more about the young artist. With Lefler's encouragement, said Hammer, Schönberg invited Gerstl to his apartment in the Liechtensteinstrasse, not far from the Gerstls' family home in Alsergrund, where he soon began regular sittings for a life-sized portrait. Schönberg was instantly impressed by Gerstl's passion and intensity, as well as his outspoken disdain for the currently fashionable painters in Vienna. They soon found they had much in common. The composer's determination to reinvent musical form was mirrored by Gerstl's desire to challenge traditional ideas of painting, and Gerstl was quickly introduced to Schönberg's tight circle of friends and pupils. They usually met in the Café Central or the Löwenbräu beer hall, just behind the Burgtheater, and included budding young composers such as Anton Webern and Alban Berg, who, at that time, were still unknown.

Gerstl was soon spending much of his time painting in the Schönbergs' apartment where the life-sized portrait of the composer was quickly completed. At Schönberg's request, Gerstl began a second, matching portrait of his wife, Mathilde, with their young daughter, Trudi. Sensitive to Schönberg's perennial financial difficulties, Gerstl gifted both paintings to the family as a token of their rapidly growing friendship. These, Hammer believed, were either still in the possession of Schönberg or his former student Alban Berg. Under Gerstl's instruction, Hammer went on, Schönberg was also learning to paint. In return, Schönberg arranged new sitters for Gerstl from his circle, including Berg's sister, Smaragda. As well as being a gifted pianist, Smaragda had a reputation for being witty and well-read, and more of a social rebel than her brother. The Bergs were an affluent family and lived in a villa in leafy Hietzing, opposite the gardens of the Schönbrunn Palace, close to Klimt's studio. Smaragda was regularly to be seen at the Löwenbräu in the company of Altenberg, Loos and Kraus, or at the Café Museum with Klimt. Although she was barely twenty, her opinions were valued in their intellectual circles. Hammer said he had never seen Gerstl's portrait of her, since it had been painted in the Bergs' villa, and, as far as he was aware, that painting was also still in the possession of the Berg family.

Turning out of the gates of the Belvedere, we cut across the south side of the Karlsplatz past the Secession building in the direction of the Mariahilferstrasse. On the corner of the Gumpendorferstrasse, Hammer stopped in front of Café Sperl and pointed upwards.

'That was Gerstl's studio up on the second floor, Herr Doktor. Lefler arranged it for him. Of course, we've just passed the Schillerplatz, so it was just a short walk from the Academy. Shall we go inside?'

Café Sperl was well known as a second home for artists, musicians, actors and singers from the nearby Theater an der Wien. We sat in one of the velvet-upholstered booths, the large mirror reflecting the traditional marble tabletops, wood paneling and brass chandeliers. A waiter came to take our order.

'At the Academy, Lefler's classes were having a noticeable impact on Gerstl's work,' Hammer continued. 'During the autumn semester, in his studio upstairs, he produced a series of small self-portrait drawings and paintings. He had started to experiment with a style influenced by the new French Post-Impressionists, which he had seen in the Secessionist exhibitions. His palette was more highly-coloured, the brushmarks more visible, the dabs and flecks of paint increasingly restless and animated.'

'As soon as the first signs of spring arrived, Lefler encouraged Gerstl to turn his attention towards working outdoors,' Hammer went on. 'His interest in plein-air painting, which we had studied years before at the summer school in Nagybánya, was soon reignited. He regularly took the cog railway from Nussdorf station near his home through Grinzing up to the Kahlenberg, where he started to paint small studies of the vineyards, fields and trees in early blossom.'

'He was spending most of his free time with Schönberg and his circle, so I saw much less of him. At the end of the spring semester I wasn't at all surprised when Gerstl told me that he had been invited to spend the summer months with them in the Salzkammergut near the spa town of Gmunden. Despite the unseasonable weather, Gerstl left Vienna in late June to join Schönberg's party on the Traunsee. He was looking forwards to the opportunity of continuing with his landscapes, and took with him his paints and a number of small boards and canvasses, which were easy to transport.'

'Did you hear from him at all while he was there?' I enquired.

'He sent me a number of letters and postcards from Gmunden, which I still have. Once the inclement weather finally turned, Gerstl said he was spending most of his days painting around the lake and that he had no plans to be back in Vienna until later in September. Eventually he returned only a couple of weeks before the start of the winter semester with more than a dozen new works. He was keen for me to see them.

Many of the paintings depicted the lake shore and lush meadows and orchards, painted in close shades of green. A few of them looked very recent, as their colours suggested the fading summer and early autumn. In these Gerstl had begun to apply the paint in a new way, largely dispensing with the final traces of his Pointillist style. The paint was now more spontaneously smeared and scraped onto the surface with a raw and nervous energy, instantly reminding me of an exhibition at Galerie Miethke, which we had visited the previous year.'

'I'm assuming that you mean the exhibition by Vincent van Gogh. Some of Gerstl's landscapes certainly recall for me van Gogh's paintings at Auvers,' I observed.

'You're absolutely right, Herr Doktor. It was the first full exhibition of van Gogh's paintings in Vienna. It obsessed Gerstl, the landscapes in particular, and he went back to see them several times.'

Feramühle
Traunstein 18

July 16th

Dear Hammer,

Nothing but rain and storms since I arrived! Because it is almost impossible to paint outside, Prillinger, the owner here, has asked me to paint his portrait. The farmhouse is on the hillside overlooking the lake just a few hundred metres from the Schönbergs. This evening we are all going for supper again at the Hois'n Wirt.

I will write again when I have managed to complete some paintings!

I hope you are in good health.

With best wishes,
Gerstl

Feramühle
Traunstein 18

August 2nd

My dear Hammer,

Finally, finally, over three weeks of wet and stormy weather have given way to something more like summer! Everyone is now arriving. The Zemlinskys are here after their honeymoon and are staying at the farmhouse next to the Schönbergs. Irene Bien is staying with them, so is Krüger. Webern arrives later in the month and it is possible Berg will also visit sometime from Villach. Diez is at an hotel in Gmunden, as Traunstein is quite remote – four kilometres on foot from Gmunden – although the steamboat makes the journey three times a day. Zemlinsky's sister-in-law, Melanie, is also here with her husband, an American artist called William Clarke Rice. It is his first visit to Europe. To help pass a miserable day, he painted a portrait of me (not very good!) but they are likeable people. He has already left again for Rome. I have started to paint outside but we have all been enjoying the sunny days rowing on the lake or walking in the mountains. Due to all the rain, everywhere is lush and green. One day we caught the steamer down to Ebensee at the southern end of the Traunsee and walked about eight kilometres for lunch at an inn between the idyllic, crystal-clear lakes of the Langbathseen.

I am becoming very restless with not painting, so next time I write, I hope to be able to tell you about some new work!

My regards,
Gerstl

Feramühle
Traunstein 18

August 26th

Dear Hammer,

Thank you for your card – I had almost forgotten Vienna! My apologies for not writing sooner but I have been very busy painting most days. Schönberg spends a lot of time working or in classes with his students, so I have had a lot of time to myself. There is a quiet path above the lake which leads directly from Feramühle to Engelgut. It's a perfect place to work undisturbed and I have painted a number of small landscape studies there. I also rowed across the lake one day and painted the view looking back from the boat towards the Erlakogel and what they call the 'Schlafende Griechin', because the contour of the mountain against the sky resembles the profile of a sleeping woman!

In the evenings I have been busy reading. Do you recall on one of our walks around Grinzing when we discussed Goethe's and Schopenhauer's colour theories? It was Schopenhauer's insight that changed my ideas about painting. Although we might describe an object as red, the colour only exists in the retina of the eye. Not in the object itself. Now I have been studying Charles Henry's 'Harmony of Forms and Colours', a major influence on the Neo-Impressionists. He supports their view of painting as the organization of independent forms and colours, rather than an attempt to copy the natural world. It reminded me of what we learned at Nagybánya with Hollósy, when painting is reduced to an assortment of shapes, tones and colours.

I am also reading Signac's own essay on colour, 'From Delacroix to Neo-Impressionism'. Do you recall when we saw his paintings at the Secession? Signac argues that the Neo-Impressionists fascination with optical effects can be taken further to an art in which colours are freed from their local and representational significance. He quotes Delacroix's theory that it is better if brushstrokes are not physically blended, as they naturally melt into one another at a given distance, giving colour more energy and freshness. The Divisionist brushmark, he insists, must be changing, alive and 'like light', rather than just simple dots, or uniform dead matter!

I have been giving these ideas a lot of thought and am trying to put them into practice with my small landscapes, using a very limited palette of mainly greens and yellows. I don't know what Lefler will make of them! But now I want to push them further.

My best regards,
Gerstl.

Feramühle
Traunstein 18

September 7th

Dear Hammer,

There is still so much to learn. I have completed over twenty paintings since I have been here but in the last couple of weeks I feel that I have at last made a real breakthrough. Now I understand that there is nothing else but the paint, the brushes and the canvas; the act of painting is like alchemy, and something has to be destroyed in order to create something new!

We are staying here for Schönberg's birthday on the 13th (and mine the following day!), so I will be back in Vienna soon after. I look forward to seeing you and showing you my new paintings!

Until then,

With my best wishes,
Gerstl

9

Café Sperl was well known for its somewhat leisurely service; the waiter finally served our Grosser Brauners on traditional oval silver trays with two small glasses of water, as Hammer continued with Gerstl's story.

'In the last couple of weeks before the Academy semester began, Gerstl took advantage of the fine autumn weather, completing some larger landscapes in and around Vienna. As well as returning to his favourite destinations north of the city around Grinzing and Nussdorf, where he painted the village church and the countryside in its golden autumnal colours, he also began to paint views of the city itself. He set up his easel on the banks of the Danube Canal, capturing the buildings on the opposite tree-lined bank of the Rossau district against an overcast September sky. The finished painting made Van Gogh's work look almost conventional.'

'Once classes began, Gerstl took his new paintings to show Lefler. Lefler's reaction was cautious, recognising that Gerstl was pursuing a radical new path, which was impossible for anyone else to follow. Privately he told me that, as far as he was concerned, Gerstl was now beyond tuition. Lefler, however, was always supportive of his students and offered to speak to the Hagenbund's selection committee about the possibility of including both Gerstl's and my work in one of their Society's exhibitions. The Hagenbund committee met here in Café Sperl. While two of my paintings were accepted, the committee flatly rejected Gerstl's as too challenging, no doubt afraid of provoking a controversy similar to Schönberg's reception by the music critics.'

'This rejection by the establishment now seemed to bind Gerstl and Schönberg together even more tightly. Undaunted, Lefler decided to approach Galerie Miethke on Gerstl's behalf. Miethke's artistic director was Carl Moll, Klimt's close friend, and the gallery had long been his exclusive dealer. Moll agreed to include a few of Gerstl's paintings in a mixed exhibition later in the year but Gerstl immediately rejected the idea, as he refused to show his work alongside Klimt's.'

Hammer drank his coffee, pausing before asking, 'Do you know the Liechtenstein Palace, Herr Doktor?'

'Yes, of course – it houses the Liechtenstein family's magnificent collection of paintings.'

'It was always one of my favourite galleries, and I used to visit as often as I could. I was particularly fond of those monumental Rubens paintings. While I was there one day that autumn, I came across Gerstl by chance in the gardens, painting a view of the palace. It was fascinating to see him at work. He had abandoned any semblance of traditional technique, and applied the paint not only with his brush but with his hands too. His concentration and intensity were mesmerising; every mark of paint he placed onto the canvas seemed as spontaneous as handwriting. Something else surprised me that day too. Gerstl wasn't alone: he was accompanied by a woman with striking dark red hair, whom he introduced as Mathilde Schönberg.'

'Was that the first time you had met her?' I asked.

'Yes, I rarely joined Gerstl with the Schönberg group. My musical tastes are far more conservative. I had met Schönberg briefly once or twice but never Frau Schönberg.'

'Did Gerstl give any reason for her presence there?'

'Not directly. Gerstl had previously told me that Schönberg spent a lot of time teaching his private students, as it was his main source of income and that when he was busy some evenings, Gerstl had accompanied Mathilde to the opera and other concerts.'

Hammer checked the time. 'My apologies, Herr Doktor, I will need to leave shortly.'

'Yes, of course. I'm more than grateful to you for taking the time to meet with me.'

'There isn't really a lot more I can tell you. Once winter set in, I was very busy working towards a government traveling fellowship. I had met my future wife Rosa, and my portrait of her won the Staatspreis. Through the Hagenbund, Lefler and his brother-in- law Joseph Urban had been asked to help with the celebrations for the Kaiser's 60th anniversary in June. In an attempt to encourage unity among the widely-diverging and increasingly discontent ethnic minorities in the Empire, the enormous parade along the Ringstrasse featured nationalities from all parts of the Empire: Czechs and Slovaks, Poles, Romanians, Italians, Slovenes, Croats, Serbs and Ruthenians. Lefler had been placed in charge of the artistic direction of the pageant and asked some of his students to help. The relationship between him and Gerstl was already strained, and when Gerstl expressed his view that the task was beneath a serious artist, there was a row and Gerstl stormed out. As a result, Gerstl's paintings were excluded from the Academy's Special School exhibition the following month. I believe that he even wrote to the Ministry of Education to complain of his unfair treatment.'

'Yes, I'm aware of that,' I confirmed. 'His letter was stamped as read and returned; it was still in his brother's possession. You are mentioned as a witness to the events.'

'That's true although I had no idea of the outcome. While Gerstl joined the Schönbergs on the Traunsee for a second summer, I left Vienna soon after to begin my scholarship in Paris, before traveling on to Berlin, Munich and Italy.'

'Did you hear from Gerstl at all after that?'

'Never again. It was his brother who told me about his tragic death. I returned for his funeral, which was only attended by his immediate family, his school friend, Waldemar Unger and me. When I went with Alois to the studio in the Liechtensteinstrasse, the paintings had already been taken into storage. Seeing them again will be a very strange experience. Have you already a date for the exhibition, Herr Doktor?'

'Sometime in the autumn, I hope. The paintings are all with my restorer, so it depends how quickly he can complete the work. I will certainly let you know as soon as I can, Herr Hammer. Your help has been invaluable and much appreciated. I am most grateful for your time.'

'I very much look forwards to it. Please don't hesitate to contact me if there is anything more you think I can do to help.'

We finished our coffees and the waiter brought our bill. When we parted outside the Café Sperl in the early afternoon sun, I turned right towards the Ringstrasse, deep in thought.

Traunstein 18
Nr. Gmunden

22nd July 1908

To the Ministry of Culture and Education,

I have been a student of Professor Heinrich Lefler's Special School at the academy of Fine Art in Vienna for five terms. At the School's exhibition which opened on the 19th of this month none of my paintings were exhibited. The purpose of this exhibition is to show the achievements of each student. Not only did I have the right to have my work exhibited, Professor Lefler commented about me to one of my fellow students: 'He is taking such a completely new path that it hard to follow him. But there's nothing more I can do for him.' By excluding my work without my knowledge or approval, I was prevented from competing in the Special School Prize, which was awarded to Herr Ignaz Schoenfeld. Professor Lefler has repeatedly declared to me, the last time only four weeks ago, that this student is completely without talent. As the Rector of the Academy has no authority here, I request that the Ministry of Education compensates me for this unjustifiable treatment.*

Richard Gerstl

**Professor Lefler made the above remark to Mr. Viktor Hammer.*

10

I had arranged to meet my old friend Adolf Loos outside the opera house. His deteriorating health had forced him to return to Vienna, where he was being treated at the Rosenhügel Sanatorium in Hietzing. He had still kept his old apartment in the Giselastrasse, a stone's throw away from mine on the other side of the Ringstrasse, but he now found it difficult to climb the six flights of steps leading up to it. Although only in his early sixties, he was physically a shadow of the man I had last seen. His thinning blond hair was slightly tinged with grey; his face, though still youthful and animated, more wrinkled. Always somewhat hard of hearing, he was now virtually stone deaf and carried an ear horn, but it quickly became evident that his humour and sharp wit had not yet deserted him.

'Otto, you look well,' he greeted me. 'Prospering, I hope. Time seems to fly as we get older. How long has it been?'

'Nearly seven years, believe it or not,' I replied, taking his hand. 'You are never in one place for long enough!'

'Claire and I have become somewhat nomadic, I must admit, but we have many homes!' he replied. 'I was here in Vienna for so long that the Austrians still say I'm one of them but then so do the Germans because I speak their language like a native. The Czechs think I'm a Czech because I was born in Brno. In France they suggested I should be naturalised because I love their country so much. And you'll remember Bessie, my English wife? She always said that I dressed better than any Englishman.'

I laughed. 'So what nationality do you consider yourself now, Adolf?'

'I belong to no country.' He smiled wryly. 'I'm a cosmopolitan, like any true European!'

At the top of the Kärtnerstrasse a small crowd had formed around a teenage boy holding a cage. Inside were two very tiny monkeys, chattering like children in high-pitched voices. They were performing extraordinary acrobatics on a pole, stopping occasionally to stare with their wide old-men eyes at their curious audience. The children were captivated; so, too, was Loos.

'Those are marmosets', said Loos. 'Many years ago I owned a similar pair. They were totally devoted to each other. During the day I used to let them run free and climb trees but they always came back home in the evening. Sadly, the female monkey caught a cold and, despite us doing everything possible to save her, she died a few days later. After that the male monkey refused to eat and just stared at the empty cage. Eventually, he climbed up onto the roof and threw himself down onto the street, breaking his neck. It was clearly a suicide', Loos declared.

We strolled down the Kärntnerstrasse, before turning into the passageway where his famous American Bar was tucked away. He had designed this tiny cocktail bar after his return from America in 1908, at the same time as he was beginning work on the building which created his reputation as Vienna's most radical and controversial architect. The façade of the gentlemen's outfitters' Goldman and Salatsch's building on Michaelerplatz was designed entirely without ornamentation. When it eventually opened in 1912, it was described as a 'woman without eyebrows', because its plain windows lacked any decorative detail. It stood in stark contrast to the baroque Hofburg directly opposite.

Above the entrance to the American Bar was a protruding prism-like construction, made of coloured glass and displaying a stylised red, white and blue American flag. Below were four rectangular marble columns and three large glass doors with brass panels. We entered through the central door, protected inside by a heavy leather curtain, into a tiny, mirrored lobby. Loos said he was still proud that it was Vienna's first American bar, and in fact Europe's first cocktail bar, importing his New World experience to the old imperial capital. But instead of concerning himself with ideas of social improvement, endorsing most architects' misguided belief that they can change the world, he had tried to create an atmosphere of intimacy, sociability and conviviality.

'The difference between me and a Bolshevik', Loos quipped, 'is that they want to turn everybody into proletarians, while I want to turn everyone into aristocrats'.

Loos preferred to sit on the high stools at the bar. He no longer drank alcohol and ordered a glass of warm milk, prescribed by his doctor, he explained, for a stomach ailment. Though famed as a skilful raconteur, he had always spoken in a very soft voice, and I struggled slightly to hear him over the noise of the bar.

'It was originally intended as a men-only bar,' Loos explained. 'When it opened, every day the place was completely full. Any women were turned away but they became very angry about not being allowed in: countesses and princesses begged to be admitted and some resorted to threats but all to no avail. It caused a sensation in the press, which of course only gave the bar a lot of free publicity. But, after a few weeks, the situation became impossible and the women finally forced their way in.'

Loos pointed at the ceiling, 'These marble panels caused a lot of trouble. The Italian engineer said they would definitely fall down and refused to put them up. He became furious and virtually attacked me. Later he was full of apologies and asked how he could make up for his behavior, so I just told him to put them up anyway. Over twenty years later they are still here.'

11

Loos had quickly become a regular visitor to the Neue Galerie. One day he came to me to say that Oskar Kokoschka, whose work he had first discovered in the Kunstschau of 1908, was returning to Vienna to visit his father, who was seriously ill. Kokoschka, in particular, had proved the *enfant terrible* of modern painting to a sceptical Viennese audience. Even before the war, his exhibitions had been met with howls of derision from public and critics alike, one of whom had described his show as a 'chamber of horrors'. He had fled to Italy, accompanied by the recently bereaved Alma Mahler, their affair causing yet another scandal. When he returned to Vienna, he was appointed to a teaching position at Eugenie Schwarzwald's private girls' school where Zemlinsky and Schönberg were both teaching but the authorities quickly stepped in and banned him from teaching altogether. As Kokoschka was desperately short of money, Loos began to fund him to paint portraits, many of whose subjects were part of the architect's wide circle of friends in the Viennese art world.

Called up in 1914 to serve in the Imperial Empire's dragoon regiment on the Russian Front, Kokoschka was seriously wounded by a Cossack's bayonet. Alma Mahler believed him dead and, by the time he was discharged from hospital, she had married the architect Walter Gropius. Kokoschka had settled in Dresden to recover his health and, according to Loos, his sanity. Still tormented by Alma Mahler's rejection, he commissioned a life-sized, chestnut-haired doll of his former lover from the Munich doll-maker, Hermine Moos. Before the doll's arrival, Kokoschka purchased a wardrobe of clothes and even secured the services of a lady's maid, a young

Saxon girl by the name of Hulda. In a fever of anticipation, like Orpheus calling Eurydice back from the Underworld, he unwrapped the doll from its packing case, only to find the cloth and sawdust dummy he lifted out was a travesty of its flesh-and-blood counterpart.

Kokoschka, nevertheless, decided to put it to some practical use as an artist's model, drawing it repeatedly and making paintings from his studies. The maid, Hulda, attended to her mistress' *toilette* and, at Kokoschka's bidding, spread rumours about the mysterious origins of the 'Silent Woman', as she soon became known. On summer days Kokoschka would take her out in a horse and carriage, often escorting her to restaurants or the theatre. His silent companion took her final leave at a champagne party thrown by Kokoschka before he left Berlin for Vienna. She circulated among the guests on Hulda's arm but, during the course of the evening, the strain of being passed from drunken hand to drunken hand took its inevitable toll: her head fell off and she lay, symbolically, in a pool of red wine.

My gallery's exhibition of Kokoschka's paintings predictably didn't pass without incident when one of his paintings was slashed by an irate member of the public. Loos immediately spotted the publicity value and informed the press that Kokoschka was so angry that he was leaving Vienna for good. He hadn't consulted Kokoschka, however, who was less than keen to co-operate. He had been spending his time painting the portrait of his friend Schönberg, who had recently remarried just months after the premature death of his first wife. Eventually, Loos and I were obliged to personally escort a rather reluctant Kokoschka to the Westbahnhof in order to ensure that he boarded the train in front of the full glare of the press photographers.

'Kokoschka is now living in Paris, where he has a major exhibition,' Loos informed me. 'As usual, it has been derided by the press. One French critic had called him a 'Boche', amongst other things. I wrote a letter to the editor, pointing out that if such a simple error had been published, then nothing they said could ever be trusted.'

When I asked Loos if he was in touch with Schönberg, he said that he had not seen him since the previous October when, accompanied by Webern, he had visited him in Berlin. Schönberg had been suffering badly with asthma in the bitter Berlin winter and was currently recuperating in Switzerland. I asked how they had first met.

'Most likely through Zemlinsky at the Café Central,' Loos replied. 'Later when Schönberg returned from his first period in Berlin, he was in desperate need of employment. I introduced him to my friend Eugenie Schwarzwald, who was a philanthropist, educationalist and patron of the arts, and had founded her progressive school for girls, mainly from wealthy Jewish backgrounds. The school was near the Hofburg in the Wallnerstrasse in a house I designed, comprising of several floors with a covered garden. Schönberg gave private lessons there in composition, while Zemlinsky taught form and instrumentation. The classes were open to all, taking place in afternoons when the school didn't require the rooms and they attracted students who became the core of Schönberg's inner circle. His enthusiasm, knowledge and charisma soon made him a magnet for Vienna's young composers. They quickly became his most vociferous supporters, and are now well-known composers in their own right, Berg and Webern, of course, in particular. Those early infamous performances of the so-called Schönberg School's music soon became a battleground between the revolutionaries and the traditionalists.'

'Particularly memorable was one of Schönberg's concerts at the Bösendorfersaal. By noon on the day of the performance not one ticket had been sold. On the spur of the moment, I got together all the money I could muster and bought every seat. I then stood in the Kärtnerstrasse and handed out them out free to whoever would take one, whether friends or strangers. That night the hall was full. Our supporters spread themselves out through the hall, so that they could deal with any disturbance in the audience. Bessie, my wife, sat up in the gallery and, at the end of the first movement, when the first hissing and catcalls could already be heard, she launched herself at the protesters, physically assaulting them.'

'Of course, the Viennese had mocked Beethoven in a similar way', Loos continued. 'His opera *Fidelio* was ridiculed. They said there must be something wrong with his ears, because what the composer clearly believed to be wonderful harmonies were, in fact, horrible dissonances. Now, less than a hundred years later, his works are recognised as one of the highest achievements of the human spirit. Are we all to believe now we have something wrong with our ears like Beethoven?' asked Loos sardonically.

12

It was Zemlinsky who introduced Schönberg to the Mahlers', Loos explained. Zemlinsky had been infatuated with Alma Mahler. After her husband's premature death, Alma's mother had married one of his old students at the Academy of Fine Arts, Carl Moll, former student of Christian Griepenkerl and close friend of Klimt. The Molls were at the centre of Vienna's cultural and artistic elite, and the young Alma's sultry beauty, privilege and quick wit ensured her an enthusiastic male following, not least of all from Klimt. Alma was also musically talented with aspirations to become a composer, and Zemlinsky was appointed as her tutor. Despite their physical contrast, he quickly fell in love with her: she was young, tall with classical good looks, he was older, short and described even by Alma as 'ugly as sin'. Nevertheless, Zemlinsky's wit, charm and deep musical erudition, and a shared love of Wagner, eventually won her round. It proved a stormy relationship: Alma's continuous social diary of parties and society balls took up so much of her time that a frustrated Zemlinsky demanded that she chose between composing or socialising, one or the other. He added sarcastically that if he were her, he would stick to what she does best – and socialise. Just as it seemed as though Zemlinsky's passion had finally overcome her doubts and she was ready to accept his proposal of marriage, everything changed. One evening at a salon in the Döbling home of Berta Zuckerkandl, Alma was introduced to Gustav Mahler, whom she had seen conducting on numerous occasions at the Hofoper. Less than a month later their engagement was making headlines in the Viennese press. When Mahler conducted a performance of *The Merry Wives of Windsor*, every eye was trained upon her as she sat in the Director's box. They were married in March; Alma, at twenty one, was almost exactly half Mahler's age. One condition of Mahler's marriage proposal, however, was that Alma gave up her own hopes for a musical career. After a period of separation, and much to his credit, Zemlinsky remained a good friend. He soon became an ardent admirer not just of Mahler's talent as a conductor but also of his far less appreciated music. Shortly before Christmas that year', Loos accompanied Zemlinsky, Schönberg and some of their pupils, to the final rehearsal for Mahler's Third Symphony in the Goldener Saal of the Musikverein. The occasion proved a turning point for Schönberg, who until then had been sceptical of Mahler's significance as a composer, if in awe of him as a conductor. Mahler, in return, became a public advocate of his 'new music', even if he could not fully grasp it. He admitted that even though he had conducted Wagner's most difficult scores and written complex music himself in scores of up to thirty staves, he was still unable to read Schönberg's score of not more than four. Nevertheless, Loos continued, the Mahlers became regulars at performances of the Schönberg circle's music. At one concert, Mahler was sat next to Polnauer, another Schönberg devotee and in contrast to Mahler a very tall, strapping man, and a public railway official, whose office was full of musical scores rather than accounting books. When the person behind him in the audience began to voice his protest, Mahler turned around and told him that he was not supposed to hiss while he was applauding. When the man replied that he also booed at Mahler's terrible music, Polnauer took direct action and hit the man very hard on the jaw. The man came back later with a knife and sliced Polnauer's face open. Afterwards he bore the scar with great pride like a war wound.

Eventually I managed to find an opportunity to ask Loos if he remembered an artist called Richard Gerstl, who had been part of Schönberg's circle at that time. Loos thought for a while before saying that he recalled meeting him only on a handful of occasions, always in the company of Schönberg.

'I think the first time was when Mahler left Vienna to take up his new appointment at the New York Metropolitan Opera,' Loos replied. 'It had come as a terrible shock for everyone. A surprise early morning farewell party was arranged for the Mahlers at the Westbahnhof from where their train departed to Paris on the first leg of their journey. Over two hundred people turned up, musicians, critics, writers and artists including Klimt, Roller, Schönberg, Webern, Berg, Jalowetz, Altenberg, Zemlinsky and Gerstl. We all carried flowers and filled the Mahlers' carriage with them. Many eyes were full of tears. Klimt summed it up for us all, quoting from Faust, 'It's all finished!' One reporter asked Gerstl for his opinion, but Gerstl dismissed him sharply, saying 'I didn't come to get my name in the press. I'm here for Mahler'. We all got together that night at the Löwenbräuhaus, just behind the Burgtheater in the Teinfaltstrasse. Even Kraus made a rare appearance there, as usual with Altenberg; they had become inseparable companions. Inevitably', Loos added, 'it soon turned into something of a fierce and slightly drunken debate about music, art and philosophy and there was something of a sharp disagreement between Gerstl and Kraus. I can't recall now exactly what it was all about but fortunately', said Loos, 'a rather inebriated Altenberg chose that moment to make a timely toast with one of his favourite aphorisms, which made everyone laugh except for Kraus and Gerstl. We all made yet another toast to Mahler and carried on drowning our sorrows until well into the early hours.'

Nussdorferstrasse 35
Vienna IX

April 21st

Dearest Mathilde,

I have spent the whole day in my studio and started another small self-portrait. Lefler wants me to paint more landscapes and thinks I'm too obsessed by my own image – narcissistic, he says. He wasn't pleased when I pointed out to him that the myth of Narcissus is usually misunderstood. Narcissus didn't know the reflection was himself, he thought it was someone else! The great Renaissance critic Alberti actually considered Narcissus, transfixed by his own reflection, the first artist (or self portraitist!).

Self-portraits are self-reflection. Reflection is a metaphor for thinking. When I study myself in the mirror, is it me or the mirror I am painting? Mirror – speculum in Latin. To speculate, like philosophers, poets and scientists.

Nietzsche says that when we try to examine the mirror itself, we detect nothing but the things reflected. When we try to grasp those things, we touch nothing but the mirror. This, he claims, is the general history of human knowledge!

Tomorrow I am going walking with Hammer up the Leopoldsberg and down to Klosterneuburg. The walk through the woods and vineyards with the view along the river and across the whole city always lifts my spirits. No doubt we will discuss more about painting! We don't always share the same opinions but he is a very good fellow.

You must come to the studio on Friday!
Your Richard

Nussdorferstrasse 35
Vienna IX

April 25th

Dearest Mathilde,

Today I went to the Zedlitzhalle to see the Hagenbund exhibition which Lefler has helped organise. You know he is one of the co-founders with Urban, his brother-in-law? Originally he had talked about including one or two of my paintings but decided it would create too much of an uproar. They would certainly have looked out of place!

By far the most interesting exhibits were some curious sculpted heads by Franz Xaver Messerschmidt. Do you remember we saw his sculptures in the gardens of the Liechtenstein Palace? He was well-known as one of the most brilliant Neo-classical sculptors of his age, teaching here at the Academy and much in demand for commissions. But these are completely different, like severed heads, probably self-portraits, each one showing an expression pulled in the mirror – laughter, rage, despair. He made them just for himself and everyone thought he had become mentally unstable. He was widely ridiculed and forced to resign but he continued to work on the heads for the rest of his life. After he died at just forty seven, sixty nine of these heads were discovered in his studio in Pressburg.

They made me think of the books I told you about by Möbius and Weininger and their theories about physiognomy. Or, even more, Schopenhauer's view that the outer man is a picture of the inner. But it has given me an idea to start a grimacing self-portrait based on one of Messerschmidt's sculptures! Better I don't mention it to Lefler!

My love,
Richard

Nussdorferstrasse 35
Vienna IX

9th December

Dearest Mathilde,

A very long night! It's nearly three in the morning and I've just returned home. But I won't be able to sleep without telling you what happened. After seeing Mahler off to Paris this morning, we all met up again later and went to the Löwenbräuhaus. Even Kraus came along with Altenberg. Once he had finished his usual evening meal of Weisswurst, Kraus started to read from the latest edition of Die Fackel. He talked about Mahler and said that it had never been harder to give an artist his proper due because overvaluation and undervaluation had become such inevitable results of the business of art that it was almost impossible for the public to see who was really great and who was just a fashionable name of the day. Countless people claim to be artists but they cannot all be geniuses. A few set the pace, the others merely imitate, he insisted. But if the many imitators want to stay in the game, they have to quickly identify the latest commercial trends in the market.

Arnold agreed with him that the genius is the future, but present and genius have nothing to do with one another. The genius lights the way, and everyone else strives to follow. You can well imagine that he was now in full flow after a few of glasses of beer. There is no great work of art, he said, which does not convey a new message to humanity; there is no great artist who fails in this respect. This is the code of honour of all great art and consequently in all great works we will find that newness which never perishes, because Art means New Art. And to be modern is enough. One has an idea, principles, taste; one knows all the critical clichés; one recognises the current trends in art; one could almost establish in advance the very problems and methods with which the art of the immediate future will have to concern itself and it is only surprising that no one has yet hit upon the idea of combining all these possibilities and concocting a guide book to the future. One cannot even claim that art is in crisis, he claimed; it is more a crisis of public taste that we are seeing today.

Even then he still kept talking. What are needed in music today, he insisted, are not so much new styles of music as men of character, men who will have the courage to express what they think and feel. A real composer like Mahler writes music for no other reason than that it pleases him. Anyone who composes because they want to please others, and has audiences in mind, was not a real artist but merely a clever entertainer, who would soon renounce composing if they could not find listeners. No artist, composer or author should accommodate his style to the audience's capacity of comprehension. The true artist must only obey an overwhelming, inner drive to express themselves and it was clear to anyone who is in the slightest degree capable of comprehending Mahler's music that he succeeded – ironic in a way because as you know Arnold has always had reservations about Mahler's compositions until recently.

Next Webern joined in as ever to support him. Before discovering Mahler, he said he yearned for a music that would be what a man writes in solitude, far from all the bustle of the world, in the sight of glaciers, of eternal ice and snow and the dark mountain peaks. The breaking of an alpine storm, the power of the mountains, the radiance of the summer sun on flower-strewn meadows, all this would be heard in the music, a spontaneous birth from alpine solitude. By now Berg, who of course loves Mahler most of all, had become quite emotional. He said that when he first heard the finale of his Third Symphony, he felt a sensation of complete solitude, as if there was nothing left in this world but this music. Mahler had given us all this and more but his reward was only derision and now exile.

Then Kraus rejoined that Art alone can express the meaning of life and moral truth. Only the artist can teach the things that matter most in life. Unity of form and content in a work of art is absolutely essential, since aesthetic form and ethical content are two faces of the same coin. Ethics and aesthetics, he claimed, were basically one and the same.

I'm afraid I couldn't stop myself contradicting him. There was a silence and I was aware that everyone was staring at me. There is no moral truth, I objected, only an aesthetic one. Ethics were merely a matter of taste. I now understood where Weininger was mistaken. What we choose to believe as right or wrong, what we think of as truth is merely what we happen to like or dislike – merely an aesthetic preference.

Not accustomed to being contradicted, Kraus was momentarily taken aback. There was a silence for a several seconds while Kraus fixed me through his monocle. Eventually, he said derisively, 'So, Herr Gerstl, now we know that you are a secret Nietzschean! Do you also believe that God is dead?!'

'What I believe, Herr Kraus,' I retorted, 'is that art contains no moral truth. It is just one individual's perception of the world – nothing more, nothing less.'

Kraus was becoming more and more irate. He raised his voice in order to be heard above the increasingly noisy table. 'All art that is not against its time is for it. Only the artist can teach the things that matter most in life,' he said. 'Art is a mission. To be concerned only with form is to pervert art.'

It was probably fortunate that Loos and Altenberg then intervened to take the conversation in a different direction. 'Art is life, life is life, but to lead life artistically is the art of life!' Altenberg exclaimed, proposing another toast to Mahler. I sat with Berg for the rest of the evening and we left together.

Now I must sleep. Meet me tomorrow afternoon at my studio! I'll wait there for you.

Richard

13

Loos and Kraus had been the closest friends and greatest supporters of Vienna's most infamous bohemian, Peter Altenberg, known to all and sundry as PA. Born Richard Engländer, Altenberg was the Bohemian's bohemian, describing himself as a professional idler and failure at everything he had tried: a lawyer without studying law, a doctor without studying medicine, a book dealer without selling books, a lover without ever marrying, and a poet without composing any poetry. He was loved by the ordinary people of Vienna, the shopkeepers, cleaners and night porters, the down-and-outs and prostitutes, whose exploitation he detested. With his bald head and drooping moustache, he was described by Kokoschka as looking like a seal. Invariably dressed in a thin loose fitting smock over checked trousers, with open sandals on his bare feet and a soft hat, PA spent the hot summer months either in the fashionable holiday retreat of Semmering, south of Vienna, or at his table in Grellinger's café at Gmunden on the Traunsee in the mountains near Salzburg. Just as much as his fragmentary writings on scraps of paper and postcards which he called 'extracts from life', Altenberg's life was his art.

In Vienna he rented a permanent room on the fifth floor of the Graben Hotel, which he called his 'nest' and where he always kept two bottles of slivovitz under the bed. Every inch of the walls was covered with drawings and photographs of the adolescent girls he adored. He was, like me, an obsessive collector and had amassed over 10,000 picture postcards, comprising an extraordinary variety of photographic images of landscapes, women, children, musicians and animals He viewed his collecting obsession as a therapy which concentrated his mind on something outside his own personality without the dangers of a full-time relationship with a woman.

From the Graben it was a short distance to his favourite haunt, the Café Central, home of the city's literary circles, where he even had his mail delivered. He shared a *Stammtisch*, a regular table, with Loos and Kraus, who were frequently called upon to bail him out of his perennial financial troubles. The Central was also home to political radicals and exiles from all over Europe, particularly Pan-Slavs and Russians, one of whom, a certain Herr Bronstein, was invariably to be found sat in the chess room. Later he became better known as Leon Trotsky. In fact, when news of the 1917 October Revolution reached Vienna, Count Czernin, Austria's foreign secretary, sarcastically asked, 'And who is going to start a revolution in Russia – perhaps that Herr Bronstein from the Café Central?'

Despite his lifestyle, PA was a passionate lover of nature and the outdoor life; a committed vegetarian, he was a strong advocate of the benefits of good nutrition and hygiene. His belief in the virtues of the simple life attracted him to visit the West African Ashanti tribal village set up in the Prater Zoological Garden as part of the 1896 World Exhibition. He soon became extremely friendly with some of the young women and children, falling in love with a teenage girl called Akole, inspiring a new series of prose sketches. He admired the tribes people as an object lesson in living in harmony with nature, seeing their culture as free of the hypocrisy and materialistic excesses that he predicted would one day prove the downfall of European civilisation.

Addicted to morphine, as well as vodka, PA gradually became an incurable neurotic, spending lengthy periods of time confined to various sanatoria, suffering from insomnia and a deteriorating nervous condition. Loos, Kraus and other friends packed him off to stay at the Lido in Venice for six months but, once back in Vienna, he soon returned to his old routine. His insistence on the benefits of sleeping by an open window even in the depths of winter proved his final undoing when he fell asleep holding a glass of wine, which spilled onto the sheets and turned to an icy damp. The resulting bronchitis led to severe inflammation of the lungs. He died three weeks later in January 1919. Kraus, the great orator, gave a moving funeral speech for his friend, the undisputed court jester of the coffeehouse literati. But PA had saved his best joke until last. Forever the pauper, living off others' generosity, his will revealed that he had accumulated a small fortune of over 100,000 kronen, which he left to a charity for the protection of children.

I had always been a great admirer of Altenberg's writing, I had only met him in person on a couple of occasions. After Loos salvaged the entire contents of Altenberg's room in the Graben Hotel from his estate, I was delighted to be able to purchase his collection of photographs, inscribed picture postcards, diaries and manuscripts. Later, once the gallery expanded, I established the 'Altenberg Room' where, together with his furnishings, I recreated as faithfully as possible his hotel room as a permanent exhibition in his honour. Loos had never seen it but even though the gallery was only a few minutes' walk away, he declined to visit, as he had suddenly become very tired.

'I would dearly love to, Otto,' he said 'but let's do it another day. All this talking has exhausted me.' I walked him back to his apartment and saw him safely up the six flights of stairs. Tragically, Loos never did see his old friend's memorial. He suffered a stroke soon after and was taken back to the Rosenhügel Sanatorium in Hietzing. When I went to visit him, he was sitting up straight in a wheelchair, motionless. He didn't speak but took my hands and pressed them to his chest. There was a look of infinite sadness of his face. I pushed his wheelchair out in to the gardens and we sat together for a time. When he tried to speak, no words came out and he gazed blankly into space while I rambled on about mutual acquaintances and old times.

Loos passed away some months later. I published a short memoir by his wife Claire. 'Adolf Loos privat', a series of brief vignettes about Loos and their life together, was a limited edition of one thousand copies and its proceeds covered the cost of his tombstone in Vienna's Central Cemetery – a plain white cube with the words 'Adolf Loos' inscribed in red. I still think of Loos almost every day when I see the sleek, glass and concrete skyscrapers of midtown Manhattan, which are rapidly proliferating, surrounding me on my way from our Central Park apartment to the gallery on West 57th Street.

14

In the first years of the century, more Jews lived in Vienna than in Jerusalem, more Croats than in Zagreb and more Czechs than in Prague. In fact, one out of five immigrants was of Czech origin. Born near Gablonz in German Bohemia in 1884, Reinhold Hanisch had led an itinerant existence as a salesman, stagehand, servant, draughtsman and artist. One day in the late 1920s, Hanisch brought his rather amateurish paintings of flowers and still-lifes to the gallery. They were of little interest to me but, noticing that the gallery also dealt in older paintings, he then offered his services as an experienced picture restorer. I decided to test him with a few paintings for simple cleaning and minor repairs: his workshop was close by in the inner city, so I could easily keep an eye on his work.

After I agreed to purchase most of his brother's paintings from Alois Gerstl with a view to an exhibition in the Neue Galerie in the autumn of 1931, I was in need of a restorer who could work quickly and at reasonable cost. I decided to entrust Hanisch with the task of cleaning and repairing them. Visiting the talkative Hanisch on a regular basis to check on his progress, I was soon well acquainted with his colourful past – he even admitted that in Berlin he had been briefly imprisoned, falsely he claimed, for fraud. But there was one story, in particular, which he was always very keen to relate to me or indeed anyone who was willing to listen.

Over twenty years previously in the autumn of 1909, under the assumed name of Fritz Walter, he had drifted through Germany and Austria, arriving in the Imperial capital as a traveling artisan. On the road, he had heard about a free lodging-house and, very short of money, decided to make his way there. His neighbour in the next bed had been living on benches in the parks for several days, where his sleep was often disturbed by policemen, moving him on. He had arrived tired, hungry and with sore feet. His blue-checked suit had turned lilac, as the rain and the 'burning' in the asylum had bleached it. Some gave him their bread because he had nothing to eat. An old beggar advised him to go to the convent in the Gumpendorferstrasse, where soup was dished out to the poor between nine and ten every morning. Hanisch's neighbour's name, he soon discovered, was Adolf Hitler.

Hanisch and Hitler quickly become good friends. He told Hanisch that he was an artist; that his father had been a small customs official in Braunau-am-Inn; that he had attended the Realschule in Linz and was well read. Now Hitler had come to Vienna in the hope of earning a living. He had already devoted much of his time to the study of art in Linz, but in Vienna he had been bitterly disappointed in his hopes.

Funded by his mother, the aspiring artist had arrived the previous September as an eighteen year old to apply for entry to the prestigious Academy of Art. Although he had passed the first test, Hitler failed the drawing examination, judged by Academy professors, including Heinrich Lefler and Christian Griepenkerl. They had suggested that his talent lay more in the field of architecture and that he ought to apply to the Academy's School of Architecture instead. He had left the grandiose, temple-like Academy on the Schillerplatz in a state of deep depression. He then found that he lacked the required academic qualifications, which meant their suggested option was out of the question. As a result, Hitler always held a particular grudge against the academic art establishment, saying they were all either artists who had failed in the real world or established artists, who gave as little of their time as possible to the Academy, while planning for an income in their old age.

Just before Christmas that year, Hitler had been obliged to return to his home town of Linz, where his mother, to whom he was very close, passed away at just forty-seven years of age. In February he arrived back in Vienna, bearing a letter of introduction from a mutual acquaintance to Professor Alfred Roller, the stage and costume designer at the Hofoper, a close friend of the opera house director Gustav Mahler and one of the co-founders with Gustav Klimt of the Secessionist Artists' Association. Living on a small inheritance and an orphan's pension, the young Hitler was still determined to realise his dream of becoming a great artist. But although he set out on three occasions to introduce himself to Roller, he was never able to find the resolve to carry it through.

15

Hitler's closest friend from Linz, Gustl Kubizek, joined him in Vienna to study at the Music Conservatory, and they shared shabby rented accommodation in the Stumpergasse. Opera was their common passion, and they saved whatever money they had for tickets at the performances at the Hofoper. From February to July, they attended every performance of Wagner's operas, queuing for hours to get the better cheap standing places on the ground floor, where the acoustics and view were best. They had seen *Lohengrin* and *Die Meistersinger* so often they knew them by heart. If Verdi or Mozart were being staged at the Hofoper, then Hitler would hope there was a Wagner opera at the Volksoper instead. Since his first short trip to Vienna in early May 1906, when he had heard Gustav Mahler conduct Wagner's *Tristan und Isolde,* there was no experience for him that could rival the opening strains of its ethereal prelude, floating up from the orchestra below.

Though Mahler's successor, the newly appointed opera director, Felix von Weingartner, had kept much of the same Wagner-dominated repertoire, he had made extensive and controversial cuts. Mahler's uncompromising attitude had not been popular amongst much of Viennese high society, who attended the opera as a social occasion and struggled with the demands of Wagner's five-hour epics. If they were late for the start or even between intervals, Mahler refused to let them in. Weingartner soon dismissed many of the Jewish singers, whom Mahler had employed, and was under instructions to make sure no more Jews were hired there. In June 1908, when Hitler and Kubizek were attending a performance of *Die Walküre,* things came to a head when a scuffle broke out in the gallery.

The purist Wagnerians demanded the opera be performed complete as written, just as in Mahler's day, while Mahler's enemies and the anti-Semites defended Weingartner and the cuts. Hitler had been furious, he told Hanisch, firmly on Mahler's side.

Kubizek was occasionally invited to perform as a viola player at private evening concerts in the homes of wealthy Viennese families. One of these was a beautiful old villa in the Grinzingerstrasse in Döbling, owned by the Jewish industrialist, Dr. Rudolf Jahuda, one of five brothers. The eldest brother, Emil, was an eminent surgeon, elegant and sophisticated; another, Georg, had followed in his father's footsteps in the printing profession and was a close friend of the satirist, Karl Kraus, and the printer of Kraus' controversial magazine, *Die Fackel.* All were assimilated Jews; Rudolf's wife, Pina, was an Italian Catholic and their two young daughters had been baptised into the Catholic Church.

Both Rudolf and his wife Pina were accomplished musicians, and loved Schubert, Mozart and Beethoven. One evening each week, the whole family, brothers, wives, children and other relatives, gathered together in their villa for dinner, followed by musical entertainment. Kubizek was regularly hired to play in trios and quartets. On one occasion, he arranged for Hitler to be invited along despite his friend's fear that he would feel out of place in his poor clothes. Because his knowledge about music was limited to Wagner, he was unable to understand very much about the ensuing conversation regarding the controversial group of young composers, centred on Arnold Schönberg. Nevertheless, he had loved the whole experience; he had been particularly impressed by the wood-paneled salon, which also served as Jahuda's substantial library.

As part of his studies, Kubizek would sometimes be given free tickets to concerts in the lavish main hall of the Musikverein, with its sumptuous décor and parade of gilded caryatids. But, apart from opera, Hitler showed little interest in any other music, especially by non-German composers. He was totally obsessed by Wagner, said Hanisch, and had read all the biographical literature, which he could get his hands on. He closely identified with the obstacles Wagner had faced and overcome, and saw his own plight as similar, remarking that Wagner, too, had been forced to fight against the ignorance of the masses around him. Wagner's notes, letters, diaries and other writings fascinated him, particularly his essay on 'The Art Work of the Future'. In discussions he loved to quote its opening phrase, 'As Man stands to Nature, so Art stands to Man'. He had an unfailing belief in the social importance and moral purpose of art.

Despite being unable to read music amd having virtually no musical training, Hitler decided to attempt to complete Wagner's opera *Wieland der Smied*, which the composer had abandoned after writing only the libretto. He worked day and night on the designs for the stage set and production while trying to persuade Kubizek to help with the music. The opera was based on one of the Nordic myths much loved by Wagner, as well as the movement of Pan-German nationalists inspired by clairvoyant and mystic Guido von List. List's philosophy combined the esoteric doctrine of Helena Blavatsky with a Darwinian racial theory, claiming that an ancient Aryan race was the original source of all world culture and religion. He also claimed that the secret of the Armanen runes, an Aryan alphabet of magical symbols possessing a deep esoteric meaning, had been revealed to him in a vision.

Hitler had acquired a copy of List's popular book *The Scret of the Runes* from the library and carried it around with him. He also soon became fascinated with List's closest disciple, the occultist Lanz von Liebenfels and was an avid collector of his magazine *Ostara*, published in Vienna. His opera however came to nothing after Kubizek left the flat in the Stumpergasse to return to Linz.

16

Hanisch suggested that, with his artist's training, Hitler could earn money by painting postcards of famous Viennese sights. Hitler thought he would never be able to sell them, as he was not well enough dressed; he was also afraid that, without a license, he might get into trouble with the police. So Hanisch offered to peddle the postcards himself. Though Hitler was a very slow painter, Hanisch began to find buyers in the local shops and taverns

Hitler mainly copied other postcards of Viennese views in ink and watercolour, which Hanisch took to art dealers and frame makers, as well as furniture stores and upholsterers, because, at the time, divans were usually designed with pictures inserted into their backs. He soon started to bring in numerous orders. It seemed as though Hitler was employed at last, his worst times over and that things were looking up. Unfortunately, Hitler was never a hard worker and Hanisch was frequently driven to despair by bringing in orders that he simply failed to fulfill.

Hanisch was mainly selling the watercolours to Jewish dealers: Jacob Altenberg in the Wiedner Hauptstrasse, who also had a branch in the Favoritenstrasse; another Jewish shop nearby owned by Landsberger; as well as Samuel Morgenstern. Morgenstern was a Hungarian Jew from Budapest, who had opened a glazier's store at 4 Liechtensteinstrasse, behind which he had a framer's workshop. Frames were easier to sell, he had discovered, if they had pictures in them. His regular clientele were the affluent Jewish merchants, doctors, lawyers and academics, who had begun to move into the elegant new tenement buildings around the Liechtensteinstrasse.

The turning point for Hanisch came one day at a small frame manufacturer in the Grosse Schiffgasse, a little street in the Jewish ghetto, where he met a dealer in antiques called Siegfried Tausky, who showed him a silhouette on gilt glass. Tausky asked Hanisch if he could produce work like that. When he said he could, the dealer gave him a piece of the glass, and he drew out a silhouette of a lady on it. Tausky then gave him a larger piece of glass, and asked him to make a 'Schubert evening concert' silhouette with a number of figures. As he did not even know who Schubert was, he turned this over to Hitler. The next day Hanisch met Tausky again, who gave him another plate to work on. He worked on it solidly for two days, and then went to get the other plate from Hitler, who predictably still had not completed it. Hanisch stayed and watched over him all the next day until he completed it. When he was finished at last, Hanisch asked him how much to charge for it, and Hitler suggested a hundred kronen. Hanisch tried to make him realise how impossible it was to get such an enormous sum; eventually, they agreed just to get as much as they could.

Hanisch reached an agreement with Tausky about the price but he was amazed to find out that he liked his own work better than Hitler's. Hitler fell very much in his esteem, since he still had belief in his partner's artistic abilities, when he made a proper effort. Hanisch lacked self-confidence in his own work and doubted whether he could continue to do work good enough to satisfy Tausky, as he did not have the benefit of Hitler's supposed academic training. Nevertheless, despite his doubts, Hanisch now began to build up hopes of freeing himself from his miserable surroundings, and his dependence on such a lazy partner.

Hitler had recently finished a watercolour of the Parliament in Vienna, which he had worked on more diligently than usual and hoped would sell in one of the better shops. As Hanisch was better dressed, he was supposed to do the rounds of these shops but, on this occasion, Hitler decided to accompany him. Again, all their attempts were unsuccessful, and they were not even asked the price. The shopkeepers just shrugged their shoulders, and one said that it was just too poor a piece of work. Hitler had expected a lot of it and became dejected, yet this time Hanisch was not able to find the words to console him. Eventually, Hitler told him to go and sell the picture on his own. He felt somewhat sorry for Hitler; he had worked for more than eight days on it. Desperate for money, he eventually got twelve kronen from Reiner, another frame-maker in the Liechtensteinstrasse; he was paid six kronen straight away, which he gave to Hitler, waiting for the six still to come as his own share.

The next day, Hanisch needed to deliver a painting of a town in Bohemia, copied from a photograph that had been ordered two weeks previously. The customer was going to take it back there as a gift, and he had promised faithfully to deliver it on time. However, when Hanisch asked Hitler for it, he gave him an excuse about being involved in some political debate. When Hanisch realised the work was still not finished, he became very angry and there was a big argument between them. For Hanisch this proved the last straw. He moved out of the Asylum and found a private lodging to work on his own.

When he went back to Reiner's shop to collect the six kronen he was still owed, Hanisch found a gentleman in the shop. Reiner introduced him as the one who had painted the Parliament picture, and the man told him to call on him at his home in Döbling. It turned out that he was a director of a bank, and he gave Hanisch a large order for more paintings. Within a few days he had delivered to him three watercolours which he approved of, and received a further large order for seventy watercolours of traditional Austrian folk costumes.

17

Just as things seemed to be looking up for Hanisch, one late afternoon on the Favoritenplatz he bumped into a salesman named Loeffler, a Jew who also lived in the Asylum, and one of Hitler's circle of acquaintances. When he asked him what news there was from the Asylum, Loeffler reproached Hanisch for having stolen a picture by Hitler. Astonished, he asked which picture he meant. Hitler, he said, claimed that Hanisch had defrauded him of the watercolour of the Parliament. When Hanisch denied it, it turned into a violent argument, during which a policeman arrived and took them both off to the police station. Because Hanisch had no identification papers, he was held and they quickly discovered that he was using a false name, which in itself was a criminal offence.

At first, Hanisch hoped that Hitler would clear up the error, and that the whole affair would sort itself out. He was taken to the Brigittenau Police Commissariat and confronted with Hitler, but Hitler, whom he had helped so often, declared that he had stolen a watercolour of his, worth fifty kronen. When Hanisch objected that he had given him his share of the twelve kronen, he denied it. He testified that Hanisch had sold the picture to a dealer in the IXth District, but Hanisch still refused to reveal the dealer's name, as he thought that, if the bank director found out that he was not the one who had painted the Parliament picture, he might cancel the rest of the order.

In court two days later, Hanisch was asked again where he had sold the picture but he still refused to give any name. His fellow prisoners had already told him that he would certainly be convicted for living under a false name, so he made little effort with his defence. Appearances were against him, and he was sure he would be found guilty. Hitler persisted in his false accusation, and, as the deal was a verbal one, Hanisch could not offer any other proof and was sentenced to a short prison term. As he was being taken away, Hanisch shouted out to Hitler, 'I will come and find you!', but he was reprimanded by the court and threatened with further punishment.

As soon as he was released from prison, his first move was to visit the picture-framer Reiner. The bank director had already been inquiring for the other watercolours, so Hanisch worked on them every day from early morning until late at night. In a coffeehouse in the Wallensteinstrasse, he met an Italian, who was living at the Asylum, who said that Hitler was blamed in the Asylum for Hanisch's misfortune. The Italian asked why he had not called him in court as a witness, as he had been sitting nearby and overheard Hitler urging him to sell the watercolour to pay their rent. He insisted that he should denounce Hitler for giving false evidence but Hanisch decided to avoid any more trouble.

The last time he had seen Hitler was in August in 1913, leaving Jacob Altenberg's shop on the Wiedner Hauptstrasse. Hitler looked smarter, his hair short and tidy, his scraggy beard gone. Hanisch left Vienna shortly after to go to back to his home town in Bohemia, before he was called up to fight in the German army. He returned to Vienna once the war was over, but, whenever he enquired of friends and acquaintances about an artist called Hitler, no one had heard of him; it was just a name like any other. Until a few years later, that is, when Hanisch read in a newspaper that a certain Adolf Hitler had set up a political party in Munich. Immediately, he went to see Altenberg, who had done very well for himself, owning a chain of four shops and taking tea every afternoon at the Hotel Bristol. He showed him Hitler's photograph in the papers, but, as Altenberg had no interest in politics, it made no impression on him to discover that this was the same Adolf Hitler that they had once known.

18

I suggested to Hanisch that he wrote down his story about Hitler's years in Vienna, partly I must admit to prevent him from telling it to me so often. He completed it in only a few weeks and handed me his hand-written manuscript for safekeeping with a view to possible future publication. By this time, Hitler's National Socialists had become the second largest party in the Reichstag. His popularity seemed to be growing relentlessly in face of the increasing credit crisis and a potential default on the national debt. As his fame increased, so did the demand for Hitler's previously worthless watercolours.

Hanisch soon spotted his opportunity to cash in, setting himself up as an expert in Hitler's paintings, claiming that because he had been his partner and dealer before the war, he knew the whereabouts of many of his paintings. He sold them mainly to unsuspecting clients, who were unaware that the majority of them had likely been forged by Hanisch himself. He even began to pass off flower paintings as being forgeries by Hitler rather than himself; he signed these paintings, flower studies in watercolour in the popular style of Olga Wiesinger-Florian, with his initials 'R.H.' in such a way that it was hard to distinguish from 'A.H.', even though Hitler had invariably signed 'A.Hitler'. He started to give regular interviews to the newspapers about his friendship with the young Hitler, attempting at the same time to validate his fakes. Inevitably, it did not take long for these stories to reach Berlin, where Hitler had now become Reich Chancellor. Not only did Hanisch's story reveal information about the new Chancellor's past that he wanted to keep hidden, but the paintings themselves were a complete embarrassment, executed with even less skill than his own. He gave immediate instructions to stop the forgeries, and Hanisch, for good.

The son of Hanisch's landlord, Franz Feiler, who was a fervent member of the Austrian Nationalist Socialist party, was asked to approach Hanisch to purchase a painting to give to the Reich Chancellor as a surprise gift. He also told him he was looking to buy any paintings by Hitler himself. At first, Hanisch offered him a genuine painting from Altenberg's remaining stock, but then he showed him three gilt-glass silhouettes, signed by Wiesinger-Florian, claiming these were forgeries by Hitler. They were, of course, actually by Hanisch himself, who had specialised in them for years. When Feiler expressed some doubts about their authenticity, Hanisch told him that his memoirs of Hitler's early years in Vienna, including evidence of these fakes, would soon be published.

Feiler purchased a watercolour of the Michaelerhaus facing the Hofburg, signed 'A.H. 1910' at a price of two hundred schillings. He paid Hanisch a deposit and delivered the painting to Hitler at his mountain retreat in Berchtesgaden, who instantly denounced it as a fake. The police in Vienna were alerted, and Hanisch was quickly arrested, tried, convicted and sentenced to another prison term. But even this strong warning failed to deter him. On his release, Hanisch only increased his output of Hitler paintings, and ever more obvious fakes were sold by a dealer called Jacques Weiss throughout Europe. In early 1938, I learned that Hanisch had been arrested again. When his apartment was searched, not only did they discover the forgeries but also a collection of material and documents about Hitler's past. Just a few weeks later, I read in the Viennese press that Hanisch had unexpectedly died of sudden heart failure, while being held in gaol awaiting trial.

19

Shortly after the Nazi occupation, the deputy director of the Österreichische Galerie, Bruno Grimschitz, whom I had known for many years, approached me. He had recently been appointed by the Nazis to acquire important works of art, particularly those in the hands of Jewish collectors. He told me that Hitler was keen to obtain a particular painting, 'Portrait of a Lady', by the nineteenth century Biedermeier artist, Ferdinand Georg Waldmüller, whom Hitler greatly admired and believed one day would be recognised as a German Rembrandt. Grimschitz was aware that I had recently borrowed the painting from its owner, Anna von Vivenot, for an exhibition in Salzburg. As security, I had given her two thousand Austrian schillings, the insurance value of the painting but, with the Nazis about to march into Austria, the exhibition had never taken place.

When I contacted Anna von Vivenot to return the painting and reimburse the money, she made excuses and, reluctantly, I was obliged to give her more time. My own situation in Vienna was quickly becoming impossible. Not only were Jews being deprived of their possessions and rights, some were now being arrested and deported. My client and good friend, Fritz Grünbaum, had been banned from performing at his Cabaret Simpl. As part of his routine he would walk out onto a darkened stage, saying 'I can see nothing, nothing at all. I must have walked into the culture of National Socialism.' He and his wife attempted to flee to Bratislava but were detained at the border. I later learned that he had been imprisoned, before being sent to a labour camp.

Under interrogation, Reinhold Hanisch had inevitably revealed the existence of the manuscript he had written at my prompting. The police questioned me a couple of times and conducted a search of our apartment. Fortunately, I had hidden Hanisch's memoirs in a stovepipe in the gallery, and nothing was found. They did, however, seize my Hudson American car and shortwave radio, as well as paintings, which they destroyed in front of my eyes. When one of the SS officers believed he had spotted another work by 'one of those Jewish artists' hanging between the bookshelves in the library, I took great pleasure in telling him that he could be quite proud if he was as Aryan as Kokoschka. But many of the artists, whose work I had promoted for over twenty years, were branded as 'degenerate', exhibiting and selling them strictly prohibited.

However, it was now clear that it was just a question of time; the decision to escape Vienna with my family was made. I decided to transfer the ownership of the gallery to my assistant Vita Maria Künstler, whom I knew I could trust. I then burned all the books, papers and manuscripts, which could have proved in any way incriminating, including a souvenir from Hanisch: a watercolour by Hitler, whether genuine or not, I never really knew.

A letter finally arrived from the von Vivenots, agreeing that the painting could be sold for six and a half thousand schillings, but only on condition that it was to Reich Chancellor Hitler himself. Grimschitz personally delivered the painting to Berlin, where Dr. Goebbels gave it as a gift to Hitler on behalf of the party. In April, I received the money from Grimschitz, and immediately paid the von Vivenots their balance of four and a half thousand schillings.

One day in June, while we were at home eating our evening meal, my lawyer Dr. Alfred Indra unexpectedly turned up at our apartment. From sources inside the Nazi regime, he had learned that a warrant was being issued for my arrest. With the remaining two thousand schillings from the Waldmüller sale, we left Vienna just twenty four hours later on the night train for Lucerne in Switzerland. In order not to raise suspicion, we took little with us. A few years earlier, I had sold my aeronautical collection there, keeping the proceeds in a Swiss bank account. I did not know until later that my wife Fanny had also hidden a small collection of gold coins in one of our bags, underneath our daughter's hair ribbons.

Once in Switzerland, I successfully persuaded Grimschitz to allow me to take out of the country a number of nineteenth century paintings, though not including works by favoured Nazi artists, which Grimschitz said must be 'sacrificed to the gods'. I was also allowed to keep my remaining collection of paintings by artists such as Schiele and Kokoschka, who were not yet considered significant enough to be included as part of the country's cultural heritage or on the Nazis' list of banned artists. Some I arranged to be sent to Switzerland; others, including all the paintings by Richard Gerstl, I left in Vita Künstler's care until the day I could return.

In Lucerne I was bitterly disappointed to be refused a work permit, and was forced to continue alone to Paris. There, I soon found empty premises, briefly re-opening the gallery as Galerie St. Etienne, the French name for Vienna's famous St. Stephen's cathedral. However, the French authorities, for no clear reason, denied permits for my family. In any case, the imminent threat of Nazi invasion was making it dangerous to remain. In order to raise enough money to escape, I sold Hanisch's manuscript to the German-Jewish historian, Konrad Heiden, who was living in exile in Paris, working on a book about Hitler's rise to power. So, in the late summer of 1939, just days before the outbreak of war, together with my wife, children and our remaining belongings, I sailed from Le Havre for New York on the SS *Ile de France*.

20

The first frost of the autumn was lying on the grass in front of the palm house, as I cut through the Burggarten to meet Alexander von Zemlinsky at Café Landtmann. I immediately recognised his diminutive figure, the habitual cigar protruding from his bird-like profile. For over twenty years Zemlinsky had been living in virtual exile, first in Prague and then in Berlin. Since those distant days of the first decade of the century when Vienna had seemed the centre of the musical and cultural world, he had watched as his hometown had been slowly reduced to the status of a provincial capital of a small Central European republic.

Landtmann was still quiet, a little too early for its regular clientele of politicians, writers, actors and students. We sat facing each other next to the tall arched window, looking out across the Ring to the university opposite. Landtmann, Zemlinsky reminisced, had been his preferred café in Vienna before the war, where he would come several times a week, sometimes accompanied by Schönberg, his brother-in-law. It was also where Dr. Freud would regularly be found on Saturday evenings, playing tarock with his friends. They were challenging and exciting years, he said, which he looked back upon with a growing sense of nostalgia. Since the death of his sister Mathilde eight years previously, he no longer had any family in Vienna but, now nearing sixty years of age, Zemlinsky was desperate to return.

Germany was in crisis: unemployment in the millions, banks on the verge of collapse and inflation out of control. Hindenburg's government looked increasingly weak and the rise of Hitler's National Socialists inexorable. Zemlinsky's position as musical director of the progressive Berlin

Kroll Opera had recently been terminated when the new government led by the German National People's Party, supported by the National Socialists, had taken away its subsidy, accusing it of promoting Jewish pessimism at the expense of Aryan, Christian culture. Just a few weeks earlier, on the eve of the Jewish New Year, Zemlinsky said Nazi gangs had attacked Jews returning home from the synagogue. He had only remained in Berlin to conduct a forthcoming performance of the Brecht and Weill satirical musical drama, *The Rise and Fall of the City of Mahagony*, whose premiere in Leipzig had caused a scandal reminiscent of his brother-in-law's concerts in Vienna before the war. Schönberg, he added, had been teaching at the Berlin Academy of Fine Arts, so that they were based in the same city for the first time in over sixteen years.

It was through him, Zemlinsky continued, that Schönberg had met his sister. In her younger years Mathilde had been musically talented but Schönberg needed someone who would take care of all his domestic arrangements and there was little room for another musical talent in the household. Although Mathilde was his opposite in many ways – she was shy while he was more of an extrovert – Zemlinsky said they had been very close and would do anything for each other. Schönberg admitted she was particularly good at restoring the peace whenever there was any conflict in the household because she invariably put others first and always tried to keep everyone happy. It was probably the Catholic in her, Zemlinsky wryly remarked, but sadly it was also her nemesis.

The head waiter, who had a rather unhealthy yellowish complexion, brought our Kapuziners. Since Zemlinsky had mentioned how he had been the victim of the rising tide of anti-Semitism, I had mistakenly assumed he came from a Jewish background but he explained that their grandfather, whose name was Semlinsky with an 'S', was a Catholic from Hungary. He had married a musician working at the Theater-an-der-Wien and moved to Vienna, where he was employed on the Schönbrunn railway, before becoming a clerk in the Imperial waterworks. After he retired, he opened a tobacco shop in the Jewish quarter of Leopoldstadt.

His son, Adolf, had ambitions to become a writer, changing the spelling of his name, as Slavs were often looked down upon in the literary world. He also added a 'von' for good measure as a sign of status.

Either because he was involved in the publishing world or, more likely, simply because he lived in the Jewish community, Adolf met and fell in love with Clara Semo, the daughter of Shem Tov Semo, a Sephardic Jew, who had moved to Vienna from Sarajevo. Together with his brother, Alexander, after whom Zemlinsky was named, Semo founded a monthly journal *El Correo de Viena*, whose name reflected the Sephardic Jews' Spanish descent. After the Sephardic Jews had been forced to convert to Catholicism or flee from Spain, many settled in Turkey, where the skills they had brought with them from producing codices and illuminated manuscripts in Granada, Cordoba and Sevilla, stood them in good stead in the developing printing and publishing industry. In Constantinople, they set up the first Ottoman printing press that thrived for over four centuries. In Leopoldstadt, the Sephardic Jews kept themselves apart from their Ashkenazic neighbours, who were largely from Eastern Europe.

Semo joined forces with a group of like-minded liberal thinkers, Zemlinsky explained, who wanted to introduce social and political change to the traditional ways. His favourite saying was 'Education is the mother of Enlightenment and Civilisation. And Civilisation is the mother of the human race'. The journal was circulated widely throughout the Jewish communities of Central and Eastern Europe, the Balkans and Turkey. When Semo returned to Turkey, he left the journal to be run by his brother with Adolf, his new son-in-law and Zemlinsky's father, who had formally renounced his Catholic religion before being admitted into the Turkish-Israelite community. He was later appointed their official Secretary – a great honour, if, inevitably, poorly paid.

In order to supplement his income, Semo took on the role as contributor and editor to the fortnightly journal *Wiener Punsch*, modeled on the satirical English magazine but aimed at an almost exclusively Jewish readership. As well as general news and financial comment, his columns included 'Professor Dideltapp', which satirised artists and the art world. He also began to write novels and short stories, often based on themes from Jewish history. His most valuable book, Zemlinsky said, and the one for which he was now best remembered, was a history of the Sephardic community in Vienna, published in 1888 in a bi-lingual German-Ladino edition.

The Zemlinskys lived in a small, cramped apartment on Odeongasse in Leopoldstadt, very close to the synagogue. Leopoldstadt had become the thriving centre of the Jewish community in Vienna. It was a time of great change, when the medieval city was demolished and the new city constructed – the municipal buildings, the theatres, the opera, the museums, the university and the stock exchange, as well as the Ringstrasse itself. Despite their financial struggles, Clara Semo brought her family up with a strong work ethic, a typically Sephardic pride in their achievements, some might say bordering on arrogance, and a strict social and moral code, ensuring that the family took care of others, as well as each other. They moved into a larger apartment in the Springergasse, as Clara was expecting another child. Tragically, the baby, Zemlinsky's second sister, lived only five weeks.

To earn some extra income they took in a lodger, a friend of the family and a keen amateur pianist, who had come to Vienna to study. He brought his piano with him and the young Alexander was sometimes allowed to play or even accompany him to piano lessons. He quickly became well acquainted with Mozart, before then discovering Beethoven, Brahms and Wagner. However, within the Sephardic Jewish community, music was still practiced solely for devotion, and he was enrolled into the temple choir, where he played the organ on high days and holidays. While the music held little appeal for him, the quality of the singing and its indication of the capacities of the human voice left an indelible impression.

When Mathilde was five, Zemlinsky continued, they moved again to Pillersdorfstrasse, nearer the Prater Park with its fairground, carousels, beer halls and pavilions. Zemlinsky attended the Sephardic School, where he studied the Torah. From there he went to the Volksschule, doing well enough academically to be accepted for the Gymnasium, where his musical talent gained him an audition for the Conservatory. He studied there for eight years, which enabled him to attend almost every significant musical event in Vienna during that period. Under the guidance of his tutor Johannes Brahms, he had also begun to compose his first short pieces, mainly sonatas, *lieder* and chamber music.

Around this time, Zemlinsky had started a small amateur orchestra, called the Musikalische Vereinigung Polyhymnia, which rehearsed in a beer cellar on the Graben. The orchestra was not large: a few violins, one viola, one cello and one double-bass. They were young and hungry for music, and met once a week to play, no matter what. At the desk of cellos sat a young man, Zemlinsky said, who maltreated his instrument with more enthusiasm than technique. The name of this cellist, he soon learned, was Arnold Schönberg. Schönberg worked as a junior clerk at a bank, but he cared little for his job, covering official bank papers with his compositions; as he joked, he was often accused of preferring musical notes to bank notes. Zemlinsky and Schönberg quickly became inseparable companions.

Schönberg's family were Jews from the eastern reaches of the Empire, who had settled in Pressburg in Slovakia. His father Samuel had arrived in Vienna as a fourteen year old to take up an apprenticeship, before setting up his own business as a shoe-maker. He enjoyed singing and became a member of a choral society. Members of his mother's family had served as cantors in Prague's oldest synagogue. In Vienna they also settled in Leopoldstadt, where Arnold was born. While he was still a young boy, the family suffered a disaster when his uncle and aunt tragically lost their lives in a fire at the Ringtheater; during the Viennese premiere of Offenbach's *Tales of Hoffmann*, a lighted chandelier had fallen to the floor and quickly engulfed the auditorium in flames, trapping hundreds of the capacity audience, many of them Jewish. Their two young orphaned daughters were adopted by the Schönbergs, joining Arnold and his younger siblings, Ottilie and Heinrich.

Samuel Schönberg opened a second business to support his increasing dependents but he was a heavy drinker and smoker. He became a victim to the influenza epidemic that swept through Europe in 1890 and died aged just fifty two, leaving Arnold, as the eldest, to support his mother and the four younger children. He handed over to his mother everything he earned and what little free time he had was spent following his passion for music. From the age of eight he had played the violin, composing his own duets, which he performed with his friends and cousins. The only musical tuition of any kind Schönberg had received, Zemlinsky said, was from his school friend Oskar Adler, who at one time was Zemlinsky's close neighbor in the Liechtensteinstrasse. Adler was a physician by profession but also an extremely talented musician, who after the war regularly played violin in Schönberg's Society of Private Musical Performances. His main interests were philosophy and astrology. Zemlinsky said he was the person Schönberg still most looked up to, and who had probably exerted the most influence on his thinking. Adler was a spiritual searcher, who had a strong belief in reincarnation and over the course of many years he had given many lectures on music and esoteric thought.

When Schönberg's employer went bankrupt, much against his mother's wishes he refused to look for another office job, determined to devote his life to music. He gained work conducting a working men's chorus in Mödling, and then a metal workers' choir in Stockerau, twelve kilometres outside of Vienna. When he hadn't enough money to pay for the fare, he would walk there and back. Their repertoire consisted partly of works by Strauss and Brahms but, more often, of folksongs, patriotic songs and political songs, since the choirs were closely linked to the growing social democratic movement. These concerts were well attended but the work didn't pay well, so Schönberg was forced to supplement his meagre income by copying and arranging better-known composers' scores for music publishers.

Although he struggled to afford even the cheap standing tickets, Schönberg became an obsessive visitor to the opera. By the age of twenty five, he had seen every Wagner opera close to thirty times. After the opera, Zemlinsky would often take him to join the regular circle of writers, artists and musicians in the Café Griensteidl on the Michaelerplatz, where his mentor introduced him as his pupil. Schönberg, however, had little time for formal learning: 'one only learns what one already knows', he confidently told Zemlinsky.

A deep friendship developed between the two young composers, said Zemlinsky, and they would regularly discuss their work with each other. Schönberg was composing every musical form imaginable: violin sonatas, duets, choruses for workers' societies and, most of all, *lieder*. None of them was published and only a few friends saw the manuscripts. His first large-scale opus was a string quartet, heavily influenced by Brahms. As Zemlinsky was a member of the Vienna Musicians' Association, of which Brahms was the honorary president, he proposed a performance of Schönberg's quartet. Despite some resistance, it was played as part of a private Association concert and made a great impression. Schönberg's name began to be a talking point in Viennese musical circles.

21

Zemlinsky invited Schönberg to spend the summer of 1899 with his family, including Mathilde, at Payerbach in the foothills of the Alps. There, in just three weeks, Schönberg composed the string sextet, *Verklärte Nacht*, a radical breakthrough for him, although Zemlinsky said he personally considered it at the time a little too influenced by Wagner. A first public concert was planned the following year with the Vienna Musicians' Association but it was rejected after a trial performance. One of the committee, the critic Heuberger, sarcastically remarked that it sounded as if someone had smeared over the score of Wagner's *Tristan* while it was still wet. From that time on, Schönberg had nothing more to do with the Association.

Inspired by Richard Dehmel's poem, *Verklärte Nach*t was also his musical declaration of love for Mathilde. In May the following year, Mathilde announced that she was pregnant. Six months later, she and Schönberg were married at a register office in Pressburg, before celebrating the marriage back in Vienna at the Protestant Church in the Dorotheergasse. Schönberg now urgently needed a regular income to support his new family.

That spring the Überbrettl variety theatre from Berlin had made its Viennese debut at the Carltheater in Leopoldstadt, playing for two weeks to packed houses. The director Ernst von Wolzogen commissioned Zemlinsky to compose music for a mime drama although it was never performed. The fashion for this type of musical and literary cabaret was sweeping through Europe, and Wolzogen was keen to sign up any new talent. Schönberg had already composed songs for the Jung-Wien Cabaret in Vienna and, on Zemlinsky's recommendation, was soon hired. He and Mathilde left for Berlin before Christmas, and their first child, a daughter named Trudi, was born there early in the New Year.

The following year the families again spent the summer vacation together on the Traunsee at Altmünster. Mathilde and Schönberg seemed happy enough, but Zemlinsky's own life, he said, was in turmoil. Obsessed by his frustrated passion for Alma Schindler, who, earlier that year, had suddenly married Gustav Mahler, nineteen years her senior, Zemlinsky was feeling distraught, cheerless and totally discouraged. By the time he finally got back to work on his symphonic poem, *The Little Mermaid*, Schönberg had completed *Pelleas und Melisande* in just a matter of weeks. He had left the Überbrettl, which was in dire financial straits and taken a position at the Stern Conservatory. His new compositions were now forging a path that even Zemlinsky was finding difficult to fully understand.

When Schönberg's teaching contract in Berlin finished, he and Mathilde were keen to return to Vienna. Zemlinsky advised against it, because, apart from the Hofoper where Mahler and Roller remained in charge, conservatism was still the order of the day in Viennese music circles. Nevertheless, when the apartment next to Zemlinsky's in the Liechtensteinstrasse became available, Schönberg and Mathilde decided to take it on. The apartments were at the rear of the building and quite dark, especially in winter. Schönberg's study overlooked the Salzergasse towards the Schubertkirche, whose bells rang out for a seemingly endless succession of weddings and funerals every morning and afternoon, while Schönberg was trying to work. When he complained about this to Mahler, Schönberg was displeased when Mahler told him just to incorporate the sound of the bells into his music.

'Living almost side by side,' Zemlinsky continued, 'inevitably we saw a lot of each other. Although like any brother and sister, we sometimes fell out, Mathilde and I would do anything for each other. The imminent arrival of their second child seemed to put even more stress on their marriage. Schönberg was always struggling for money, scraping a living with a handful of private students and teaching part-time at the Schwarzwald School. His Berlin publisher had refused a further advance as they saw little commercial future in his works and his account with them was already overdrawn. The premiere of his latest work *Pelleas und Melisande* at the Musikverein in early 1905 had received particularly hostile reviews – one critic cruelly suggesting that he should be put in a mental asylum, keeping any staff paper out of his reach. He applied for the post as Director of the Vienna Choral Academy but was rejected. With one young child and another on the way,' said Zemlinsky, 'Mathilde grew increasingly depressed.'

22

In the meantime, Zemlinsky had also resigned from the Musicians' Association, taking up a position as Musical Director at the new Volksoper. He and Schönberg soon set up a rival society, dedicated to the cultivation and promotion of contemporary music, which encouraged totally free expression of artistic individuality. Their new music society arranged three concerts at the Musikverein for its first season, including the Viennese premiere of Richard Strauss' *Symphonia Domestica*, conducted by Mahler, and another evening devoted entirely to Mahler's orchestral songs. Any doubts they had harboured about Mahler's music were soon forgotten when they were invited to attend the final rehearsal of his Third Symphony. Zemlinsky had never heard music of such power and profundity. Like everyone present, they understood that they had witnessed a major event in the history of modern music.

Mahler had accepted the post of Honorary President of the new Association, and they became regular guests at the Mahlers' home. At first, Alma wasn't much impressed by Schönberg's shabby clothes but Zemlinsky told her not to judge on appearances, as the time would come when the world would have a great deal to say about him. Zemlinsky's long relationship with Alma Mahler, as she now was, had been the cause of the loss of the close friendship he had once shared with Melanie Guttmann, a student at the Conservatory, who had sung with the Polyhymnia. For a short time they were engaged to be married but his desire for Alma made the situation impossible, and Melanie eventually left for America. Still reeling from Alma's sudden marriage to Mahler, Zemlinsky turned towards Ida, Melanie's younger sister, whom he married in 1905.

In its next concert, the new music society premiered Zemlinsky's *The Little Mermaid* and Schönberg's *Pelleas und Melisande*. Both called for a huge orchestra and the costs were extremely high. Zemlinsky originally intended to conduct the Schönberg piece but it completely baffled him and Schönberg decided to conduct it himself. At rehearsal one day, Zemlinsky said, Mahler, who stood in the middle of the hall in his winter coat and fur cap, suddenly called out, 'Where is the second English horn? I can't hear it!' There was a bemused silence, before someone replied, 'He isn't here today!' It was little wonder Schönberg hadn't noticed, said Zemlinsky, the score was so complex and densely orchestrated that it was very hard to distinguish the principal melodic lines. During the first public performance, while *The Little Mermaid* was well received, the audience became restless in Schönberg's piece and some left noisily, while others stayed to whistle or yell their disapproval. The Association's third concert scheduled for the Musikverein never took place; the exorbitant cost of this ambitious project had broken the bank. They remained close companions, however, and Schönberg was an invaluable help in Zemlinsky's next project, an opera called *Der Traumgörge*. Indeed, when Mathilde bore their second child, a boy, he took his name from the main character, Georg, who was invariably known as Görgi or Görgl.

23

'Two significant events took place around this time,' Zemlinsky continued. 'Firstly, in the spring of 1906, at one of Mahler's concerts – I think he was conducting *Tristan* – Schönberg and I were approached by a young artist, who asked if we would sit for portraits. We had seen him at several other concerts and he was clearly a passionate follower of the new music. He told us he had approached Mahler to paint his portrait but Mahler had declined. The young man introduced himself as Richard Gerstl. Schönberg checked with his friend Lefler, who was Gerstl's tutor and said he was extremely talented. Schönberg soon invited Gerstl to his Liechtensteinstrasse apartment, where he painted life-sized portraits of Schönberg and my sister. As Schönberg was keen to learn to paint, Gerstl also started to give him basic tuition.. It wasn't long before he was a fixed member of our social circle, regularly accompanying us on Sunday excursions in the countryside and evenings in the cafes and beer cellars. The following summer Schönberg invited him to join family and friends for the summer vacation on the Traunsee.'

'Secondly, the complex politics of Vienna's music circles turned against me. I had started to feel restricted by the commercial ethos of the Volksoper, and when Mahler asked me, in that same spring, to supervise rehearsals for *Der Traumgörge*, I was delighted. I was offered full-time employment at the Hofoper and, needless to say, leapt at the chance. However, in September just before the score of my opera was due to be published, Mahler read it through, apparently for the first time, and ordered sweeping changes. A new libretto had to be published and forty pages of vocal score re-engraved – all at great cost. The premiere had been set for early October, so I was frantic with production meetings, design conferences and musical discussions. The orchestral parts had all been completed and copied, the sets designed and built and rehearsals were at an advanced stage, when, out of the blue, disaster struck.'

'There had been rumours circulating in Vienna for some time that, due to constant backstage intrigue and arguments, Mahler was considering resigning from the Hofoper. These rumours had been neither confirmed nor denied publicly. Mahler's enemies accused him of constantly overrunning his budget, and he had become tired of the personal attacks from court circles and the anti-Semitic press. Behind the scenes, it transpired, they had already been desperately searching for a replacement. Only two days before the premiere of my opera, the Kaiser signed the official document, which terminated Mahler's employment. As far as I was concerned, it was a total calamity.'

'Felix Mottl, Musical Director of the Munich Opera, had been approached to replace Mahler but declined. They turned to Felix Weingartner, who had been the Director of the Berlin Hofkapelle for over fifteen years,' Zemlinsky went on. 'Weingartner's task was to make radical changes and distance himself from the former Director's policies. As a close friend and colleague of Mahler, I was an obvious direct challenge to the new regime. Without even reading the score, Weingartner ordered the premiere of *Der Traumgörge* to be cancelled. Disappointingly, it remains unperformed to this day.'

Zemlinsky's position at the Hofoper quickly became untenable, especially as Weingartner was unwilling to trust him with conducting any other repertoire performances. His contract was inevitably terminated, although it was agreed that he was to be paid until finding another permanent position elsewhere. He worked temporarily as guest conductor back at the Volksoper, which under Rainer Simons had achieved a far greater critical respectability. He conducted the opera *Ariane et Barbebleue* by French composer Paul Dukas, which proved a significant critical success for the Volksoper.

'Five weeks after the premiere of Dukas' opera,' Zemlinsky continued, 'my wife Ida gave birth to our first child, Johanna. The first few weeks proved difficult as the baby, soon known as 'Hansi', suffered a serious illness. In June, she improved a little and we packed our bags for the summer vacation by the lake near Gmunden in the mountains outside Salzburg, where we met up with Ida's sister Melanie, visiting from America with her new husband, the artist William Clarke Rice. As in the previous year, we joined Schönberg and his family, as well as Wellesz, Krüger, Webern, Jalowetz and others, including Gerstl.'

Nussdorferstrasse 35
Vienna IX

June 6th

My dear Mathilde,

I am trying to keep busy by starting a portrait of Henryka Cohn, a friend of S. Have you met her? She lives with her family in the Esterhazygasse and teaches music. Her father knows mine, as they are both stock market investors; he made a lot of money from the dairy business. I have been thinking about a painting which will be my version of a Klimt! That would amuse me. I am trying to complete it before I leave for the Traunsee.

Werther's words keep going around in my head, 'The things I know, anyone can know – but my heart is mine and mine alone.'

I miss you so much already. Last night I dreamt about your pale white skin, your voice, your soft red hair…another three weeks is too long to wait!

All my love,
Richard

Preslgütl
Traunstein 24

June 10th

Dearest Richard,

I've armed myself with all the courage I can but please be patient with me. I know Arnold, and I won't be safe from him for even a minute; he will force me home and there will be no use arguing. Please for the sake of our love, don't let that happen! It would destroy all of our happiness.

When it is absolutely necessary, you'll see that I am brave and won't waver. I am so afraid you will think that I am being obstinate! Turning you down has never been more difficult – your every wish is mine.

I just want to kiss you and tell you that I love you with all my heart

Your Mathilde

Nussdorferstrasse 35

June 12th

Dear Mathilde,

I went over to give S. his painting tuition as usual. I have never understood how he always drums into Berg, Webern and the others how they need to study the language of music from the great masters before they can express themselves but then thinks he can instantly become as great a painter as he is musician. His drawings are direct and do have a certain charm but they are very primitive. I asked him why he was so determined to paint when he is already the greatest composer alive. I doubt he really hears me – he is always so very stubborn. We talked for a couple of hours about his ideas for a new String Quartet based on Stefan George's poems which he plans to work on during the summer. I told him about my painting of Henryka. When I left, he asked me if I had heard from you – I said just a card.

You mustn't be afraid. You know I will wait for you!

All my love,
Richard

Preslgütl
Traunstein 24

June 13th

My beloved Richard,

Yesterday was a blazingly hot day, followed by a terrific thunderstorm with sheets of rain. This morning the mountain air was icy cold but now the sun is even stronger. I long for the cool green lake. I imagine us swimming out into the waves and then back to shore and lying in the grass to dry in the sun – to taste everything our senses desire – your white body, your fragrant warm breath on mine. How short the rest of the day would seem. Then the evening comes, the lanterns go out and only the light of a candle shines here and there through the green shutters. All sounds subside and there is just the gentle chirping of the crickets and continuous rippling of the lake outside the door. Then I would open the door to your room and there would be nothing to part us before we fall asleep in the blissful arms of love.

Your Mathilde

Nussdorferstrasse 35
Vienna IX

June 15th '08

Dearest Mathilde,

Today I went over to see Berg. He has asked me to paint him. He hadn't been well (not unusual!) but fortunately he was feeling somewhat better. Of course he was obsessed with the latest edition of Die Fackel. *Kraus reviewed the Kunstschau exhibition, describing Klimt's models as having the pallor of professionally misunderstood women! Berg can't understand why Kraus is so against Klimt. We walked through the Stadtpark and had coffee on the terrace of the Kursalon, before visiting the exhibition again. There weren't as many people, so it was easier to have a good look round. But when we got to the two rooms devoted to Klimt's paintings they were full of people. With those Hoffmann frames and all that gold, Altenberg was right when he said the exhibition is like worshipping at the Klimt Church of Modern Art!*

The only things that really interested me there were a few watercolours by a student from the School of Applied Arts called Kokoschka. He must be Czech, I suppose. It was funny – somebody pointed him out to us but when I went over to talk to him, it turned out to be his younger brother!

Did I tell you that Berg won't be able to come to the Traunsee this year? It's a shame but he has to go to the family estate in Villach for the summer. I'm hoping to be with you by the end of the month. I still have to arrange to send my canvasses – this time I want to paint some larger works.

How are you spending your days? Do you think about me at all? Write soon!

My love,
Richard

Preslgütl
Traunstein 24

June 17th

My dear Richard,

I'm sorry I haven't written to you for a couple of days now, and I suppose you are mad at me, aren't you? But it wasn't really my fault. One day I had to go into Gmunden to shop; of course I spent too much money and Arnold is mad at me as well. We went with Krüger and Irene to Grillinger's, where we saw Altenberg at his usual table. Then I had to move mother's things into the apartment next door at Engelgut. You remember that was where we stayed last year. I have managed to rent it for Alex and family, and mother is going to stay with them.

Please keep your spirits up for me. I am so worried about you because you let everything affect you so, and that does you no good. How much you have to suffer for me! I will never be overcome by weakness again; I am not afraid any more – my love gives me strength for everything. Take my hand and I'll go with you wherever you wish and will never abandon you; you must stay courageous and steadfast, too. One day we will be very happy together, inexpressibly happy!

In the evenings, once the children have gone to sleep, I have been reading the wonderful book of Rilke poems you gave me – I have read them so often that I think I almost know them by heart. You won't be surprised which one is my favourite!

Yes, I long for you. As I move near
To you, I lose myself and feel no fear.
Just like you, no more will I contest
All those things in me that appear
Eternal, constant and best.

...All those times when I was quite alone,
Giving nothing away, letting no-one know,
My silence was the quiet of the stone
Over which the rippling waters flow.

But now in these first weeks of spring
Slowly something inside me has broken
Which in those dark years I kept within,
Something which you have awoken.
My whole life I am ready to give away
To someone who knew not how I was yesterday.

Forever,
Your Mathilde

Nussdorferstrasse 35
Vienna IX

June 20th

Dearest Mathilde,

Today I finished the portrait of Henryka Cohn. She is wearing a white dress, with her head half-turned – just like the Klimt portrait of Fritza Riedler in the Kunstschau! But, as you can imagine, my painting could not be more different. I have used much bolder colour than before – she is sat on a red and black sofa and her figure is contained within a wavering deep blue line. While I'm on the Traunsee I will paint more paintings like it – and you will be able to model for me!

I called on S. this evening but he was very busy decorating the children's room. He says he's travelling early next Saturday but I told him I can't leave till later in the day.

Until then!

My love,
Richard

Preslgütl
Traunstein 24

20th June

Dearest Richard,

I am looking out of the window at the lovely deep blue water, the mountains behind, the sun is shining. The steamboats with their red paddle wheels are happily going back and forwards across the glistening lake. I keep telling myself 'A week from today, a week from today!'

Have I told you that inevitably Alex and family arrive the same weekend? The baby has been quite ill and Alex is in a bad mood. Then Webern (unfortunately) is coming up from Ischl for a couple of days too. But we must find a way to have some time alone!

All my love
Mathilde

Nussdorferstrasse 35

June 23rd

Dearest Mathilde,

I have just come back from Grinzing, I went to a Heurige there this evening with Hammer. I doubt I'll see him again for a while – he has won a travelling scholarship and will soon be going abroad. It felt wonderfully secluded there, like in a fairy tale, with the lanterns glowing and all the quiet gardens and overgrown lanes, where you hardly meet a soul. We sat at an outside table; the garden was lush and green with leaves swaying in the warm summer night breeze. Such a wonderful contrast to the grey houses and hot noisy streets of the city! I'm looking forwards to breathing the mountain air. But not as much as seeing you again!!

Richard

Preslgütl
Traunstein 24

24th June

Dearest Richard,

There is something I must tell you! I can hardly believe it! As it was a warm sunny day I walked up to the Hois'n for lunch with the children. We sat at a table with a local couple, who were interested in music and started talking. They told me that on the western shore at Altmünster there is a large villa once owned by good friends and patrons of Wagner! The villa, they said, is called the Traunblick as it looks directly back across the lake to Traunstein and the Schlafende Griechin – exactly the view you painted last year when we rowed across the lake! The gardens of the villa run right down the cliff to the shore and the rumour is that a 'Wagner Grotto' has been created there. The wife, they said, passed away just a few years ago but it was claimed that Wagner had set some of her verses to music. Then, as soon as I mentioned the name Wesendonck, they instantly recognised it! You gave me the Schott piano music for my birthday, 'Five Poems for a Female Voice'! Now I love those songs almost more than 'Tristan'. When I'm at home on my own, I often play them. 'In the Greenhouse' is still my favourite. That same fateful theme as the Prelude to Act III. 'Yearning with desire you open your arms out wide. And trapped in your delusion embrace only the emptiness of the desolate void. How well I understand, poor plant, we both share the same fate. Though bathed in light and splendour, here is not our home.'

When you come, we must go back there and see if we can find the grotto!

All my love,
Mathilde

24

'Do you mind if I smoke, Herr Doktor?' We were sat in my office.

'Not at all, there's an ashtray on the desk. And coffee is on the way.' I had already noticed that a strong aroma of tobacco and coffee seemed to follow Zemlinsky.

'Extraordinary, just extraordinary,' he remarked thoughtfully, lighting up his Zechbauer cigar. 'Looking back, I can now see none of us really understood Gerstl's paintings. How has your exhibition been received?'

'Gerstl has been acknowledged as a major discovery, I'm delighted and rather relieved to say,' I replied. 'One reviewer called him 'a Viennese van Gogh'; another deemed him a genius on a level with Klimt, Schiele and Kokoschka. No artist in the world at that time, it proclaimed, had ever painted like this modern Austrian Master. As a result, I have been able to confirm a travelling exhibition for early next year in Berlin, followed by others in Munich, Cologne and Aachen.'

'Gerstl would never have thought it possible. No-one liked his work. It was really only Schönberg who believed in his paintings, even though he would never admit that now.'

'Do you remember very much about the paintings at the time?'

'Not a great deal, I'm afraid, Herr Doktor. It seems like another lifetime. I have to admit that I wasn't really thinking about them. But I was aware that Gerstl had wanted to paint my portrait for some time and there was little excuse on the Traunsee not to pose for him. He had already painted Schönberg, Jalowetz and Berg, as well as various others in our circle.'

'The weather on the Traunsee had turned quite hot and humid, so we arranged to meet early one morning in front of the farmhouse on the lakeshore, before I went off for my regular morning walk. I was surprised by the size of the canvas Gerstl brought, painting on the reverse of a canvas he had already used. It took him less than a couple of hours, working very quickly with long brushes and a palette knife, squeezing the paint straight from the tube. I'm afraid I paid little attention to the finished result, as I wanted to get on my way. I was very distracted at that period and needed time alone to think. I had just lost my position at the Hofoper and our baby daughter Hansi had been quite ill. Mother was staying with us in our farmhouse, as Mathilde said she had looked after her for long enough and once Arnold arrived, she didn't have room. Apart from which, there was noticeable tension between her and Schönberg. They still had serious financial worries, and it was obvious that Mathilde and Gerstl had become close. I was there rather reluctantly and looked for an opportunity to leave as soon as I could.'

'How were things between Gerstl and Schönberg?'

'Cordial enough from the outside but most of Schönberg's students were there – Horwitz, Webern, Krüger, and Jalowetz, as well as others coming and going from time to time. They spent a lot of time together discussing music – Schönberg had installed a piano at the farmhouse. But Mathilde was usually excluded and sometimes she would come out with us. Gerstl usually went out on his own for the day, painting around the lake.'

'Gerstl and Schönberg were quite similar, both rather obsessive and competitive characters. The farmhouse had a small rowing boat for tenants' use and we would often row across the small bay to the 'Hoisin' for lunch. I remember one day Schönberg decided he would swim across instead but the Traunsee, being a glacial lake, can be quite cold even in summer. He only got so far before he started to struggle and we had to row over to pick him up. It caused some amusement but Schönberg was highly embarrassed.'

'Even with his students, there was frequently some rivalry. He and Webern had recently fallen out over the choice of Stefan George's poems, as it was Webern, while working on setting poems from *Das Jahr der Seele*, who had introduced Schönberg to the poet's work. Shortly afterwards at a concert at the Musikverein, including *Lieder* by Schönberg, Mahler and myself, Schönberg previewed his first composition based on one of George's poems from exactly the same book. While Webern was unable to publish his songs until later that year, Schönberg was inspired by George to compose his most radical work yet. His most recent compositions had already seemed to challenge the limits of traditional music but now, in that summer on the Traunsee, he went beyond that. This was music I thought which would either never be played or would change the course of music history forever.'

'Did he talk about his ideas?' I asked.

'All the time, especially with Gerstl; music must never suggest meaning or thoughts, he now believed, and should be uninhibited by logic, completely eliminating the conscious will. An artist must express themselves directly out of an inner compulsion, not an arbitrary stylistic choice. Art, he used to say, comes from 'I must, not I can'. What you compose should be as obvious to you as your hands and your clothes. Although no new technique in the arts is created that has not had its roots in the past, he insisted it was the duty of the artist to tell you what you do not know, have not heard or have not seen.'

'Mahler had confidentially admitted to me before he left Vienna that he struggled to understand Schönberg's ideas. Although I had always recognised that he possessed a brilliant and enquiring mind, even I was beginning to feel left behind,' Zemlinsky admitted. 'Schönberg and Gerstl, on the other hand, seemed to drive each other on.'

'While Schönberg was occupied during much of the day with his music and his students, Mathilde was free to model for Gerstl and he had painted some canvasses of her in the garden. Towards the end of the month, Schönberg took a break from his own work and under Gerstl's instruction, started to paint again himself. Aided by Gerstl, he painted a small picture of Trudi. Then he suggested that Gerstl painted the whole family together and Gerstl readily agreed.'

'It was a particularly warm day when Gerstl set up his easel in the garden of Schönberg's farmhouse. There was no preparatory drawing and he immediately covered the whole canvas with paint in a rough manner. He worked quickly and silently, lost in concentration, squeezing the paint straight from the tube, those scraped and dabbed blues, smearing hot reds and pinks onto the canvas with his long brushes, a palette knife and even his fingers. I've been looking at it again for a long time downstairs.'

'The following day Gerstl asked if six of us would model for a larger canvas, a group portrait with Ida and me, Schönberg and Mathilde and Karl and Mizzi Horowitz. What struck me as curious was how he arranged the composition, with Schönberg and Horowitz standing at the back, and such a distance between Mathilde and Schönberg. As you can see, Herr Doktor, the final result was even more radical.'

'Yes, the paint is even thicker, the technique wilder, the image more distorted, and the colours more discordant and abrasive. It sometimes looks to me as if Mathilde's face is smeared with blood,' I remarked. 'Of all Gerstl's work, I find that painting the most disturbing. It's almost unimaginable it was produced at that time. It has no precedent I can think of – much like Schönberg's music.'

'In fact he painted just as Schönberg composed; both worked a feverish pace, with total confidence and without correction, fully controlled but at the same time relying on their intuition, almost as if obeying some laws which had still to be written.'

'That's a good way of putting it. It's obvious that they were inspiring and challenging each other,' I remarked. 'Both appeared to want to strip everything back to its most basic form in order to express complex emotions as directly as possible.'

'Sometimes,' mused Zemlinsky, drawing deeply on his cigar, 'I wonder if Mathilde was not caught in the middle of their private battle. I was beginning to find the atmosphere there tense and uncomfortable. Fortunately, the Mahlers had returned from New York for their usual summer vacation in the Dolomites and invited us to visit them at their house in Toblach. We left in mid-August, leaving the Schönbergs with only Gerstl, Krüger and Irene Bien for company.'

There was a light tap on the door, as Vita entered to ask if more coffee was required.

'My apologies,' said Zemlinsky, looking at his watch. 'You'll have to excuse me. I need to get back to my hotel, as I am due at the memorial service for Schnitzler soon. Fortunately, I am staying just around the corner at the König von Ungarn hotel. You would be more than welcome to join me there this evening for dinner, Herr Doktor, if you would like to continue our conversation.'

'That is more than generous, Herr Zemlinsky. I'd be delighted.'

'Shall we say eight o' clock?' Zemlinsky asked, as he picked up his hat and took his leave.

25

I found Zemlinsky waiting for me in the reception area of the König von Ungarn, an almost empty glass of whiskey on the low table in front of him and the inevitable cigar in hand.

'Our table is ready, I believe, Herr Doktor. Shall we go through?'

The maître d'escorted us to our candle-lit table in an alcove of the vaulted cellar of the restaurant, known as the Mozartstüberl, since the composer had written his famous comic opera *The Marriage of Figaro* while living in the rooms directly above. As a waiter came to the table to bring us menus, Zemlinsky immediately ordered a bottle of Blaufränkisch red wine.

'How was the memorial?' I asked.

'I doubt that Schnitzler would have approved,' Zemlinsky replied. 'Did you ever meet him?'

'Unfortunately not, though I greatly admire his writings. How long were you acquainted?'

'It must be more than forty years. I was a young music student and Schnitzler was about ten years older than me, a prominent member of the Jung Wien literary group, including Bahr, Altenberg, Beer-Hofmann, Kraus, Felix Salten and the young Hofmannsthal. We met regularly at the Café Griensteidl. I would go there sometimes with friends from the Conservatory and we soon got to know each other. Most of us were Jewish, all young and rebellious with strong opinions, obsessed with women and the latest ideas about art.'

'Kraus was highly critical though.'

'He fell out badly with Bahr and soon moved to the Café Central. From that time on, he started to satirise the Griensteidl group not only for the way they wrote but also the way they acted and dressed. After the cafe was torn down in the rebuilding of the Michaelerplatz, he wrote a mock obituary, renaming it Café Megalomania, which so enraged Salten that he sought him out at the Central and punched him on the nose!'

The waiter arrived to bring the wine and take our orders; we both chose the Nudelnsuppe as a starter, while I decided on the Tafelspitz as a main course and Zemlinsky ordered the Goulasch.

'This is why I stay at this hotel', he joked, 'home from home! A return to my Hungarian roots. Prost, Herr Doktor! To Schnitzler.'

'Prost, Herr von Zemlinsky!' I replied, raising my glass.

'Olga, Schnitzler's much younger wife, was a singer, and I helped her in the early stages of her career,' Zemlinsky went on. 'Schnitzler then wanted me to compose the music for one of his plays but it never happened. We stayed in touch however and he would sometimes attend performances of my music here. He and Olga divorced, and after I moved away, we largely lost touch. I hadn't seen him for nearly ten years but Olga invited me to come. She told me he never really recovered from their daughter Lili taking her own life a couple of years ago. She was only eighteen and not long married. Schnitzler was devoted to her.'

'It's a question for Dr. Freud – to explain why so many young Viennese have taken their own lives,' I remarked.

'I have known Freud for many years – from the time when we were both regulars at Landtmanns. Of course we shared a great passion – our addiction to cigars! I have discussed this matter with him. Freud claims that thoughts of suicide are murderous impulses against others redirected on oneself. One might say murder through mistaken identity. Mahler consulted him after Alma left him; so did Berg, as well as his sister Smaragda, who tried to commit suicide when she was still young.'

'But never Gerstl?' I asked.

'I very much doubt Gerstl thought he had any problems that could be cured by psychoanalysis,' Zemlinsky replied.

As the waiter brought our soup, Zemlinsky asked, 'Tell me, Herr Doktor, what is it exactly that you are trying to find out about Gerstl?'

I thought for a moment. 'I completely understand, Herr Zemlinsky, if you would prefer not to talk about it and I appreciate everything you have told me. But I would be grateful if you could throw any light on what happened between him and Arnold and Mathilde Schönberg. From what you and others have told me, as well as the letters Gerstl's brother gave me, I am naturally aware of some dramatic event which took place on the Traunsee. It seems to me highly likely that it is the key to the tragedy which followed.'

Picking up his glass and examining it against the candlelight, Zemlinsky swirled the wine around before drinking. 'Herr Doktor,' he went on, 'you must understand that Schönberg has been my closest friend for over thirty five years, even though we have had some ups and downs. When my sister passed away about eight years ago, I was very upset when Schönberg remarried so quickly. She had been ill for a long time and had become so withdrawn she was known as 'the silent woman'. In many ways, she never fully recovered from those events you refer to. But Mathilde used to confide in me and that often made my relationship with Schönberg difficult. Although we have not seen much of each other in recent years, we have remained close colleagues and good friends. What you are asking me to tell you I have never told anybody. But since you contacted me, I have given the matter a lot of thought. Both Gerstl and Mathilde are long gone. And now I feel it is time that their story is told. If I don't, who will?'

'Herr Zemlinsky, you can rest assured that anything you tell me will be treated in total confidence'.

'Thank you, Herr Doktor. Our meeting today has already confirmed to me that I am able to rely upon that.'

One waiter removed our empty bowls while another brought our main courses. Once our wine glasses were refilled, Zemlinsky returned to the events of the fateful summer of 1908.

26

'In Toblach the Mahlers had rented a large farmhouse with numerous guest rooms for the summer. They had sold their summer house in Maiernigg, as it brought back memories of the tragic death of their young daughter Putzi there from a scarlet fever epidemic the previous year. Mahler had doted on her but Alma always believed he had tempted fate by setting the five Rückert poems *Kindertotenlieder* and never really forgave him. In Toblach Mahler employed a carpenter to build a small shack in the large gardens where he could work in peace. Alma wanted company however and invited a stream of guests from Vienna which began to aggravate Mahler, since he was busy working on his first composition in a couple of years, another song cycle which is now known as *Das Lied von der Erde*. Ida and I decided not to stay long and soon returned to Vienna.'

'We had only been back in the Liechtensteinstrasse for a couple of days when late one evening there was a knock on the door of our apartment. The baby was asleep and Ida had already retired for the night. I was still up in my study with a nightcap and naturally a last cigar. When I opened the door, I was surprised to find Mathilde, as I hadn't expected them back for another couple of weeks. She looked tired and distressed; her eyes were red as if she had been crying.'

'What's happened? Are you all right?' I enquired.

'Alex, I'm sorry but can you lend me some money for a few days?' She came into the hall.

'I can't stay,' she added, 'I've just come back to collect some clothes. Richard is waiting downstairs for me.'

'Richard?' I repeated. It dawned upon me. 'You mean Gerstl? Where are Arnold and the children?'

'Still in Traunstein, I can't explain now,' she replied. 'I'll come and see you in the next couple of days,' she promised, hurriedly disappearing down the stairs and into the night.

'The following evening Schönberg arrived back with the children. I had never seen him in such a state – he was fraught, emotional and confused. Ida put the children to bed while we sat in his study. I poured drinks for us both and he recounted what had happened just two days earlier. That morning was warm and humid, he said, so he had suggested they all take the early steamer into Gmunden. Krüger, Irene Bien and my mother wanted to go along but Gerstl had shown no interest, as he wanted to paint for the day. As they were getting ready to leave, Mathilde said she felt tired and a bit off colour, so would prefer to stay and have a quiet day. She told them to go without her. After they had done some shopping in Gmunden for an hour, Trudi also said she felt unwell. There were only three steamers a day direct to Traunstein, so Schönberg decided to bring her back on the lunchtime boat, leaving Georg with his mother. Arriving back at Preslgütl, there was no sign of Mathilde downstairs, so Schönberg assumed she was upstairs resting to escape the midday heat. He found the bedroom also empty though the bed was unmade and some of her clothes were scattered across it. He took Trudi to her room and put her to bed and went into his work room, whose veranda overlooked the enclosed private garden at the back of the farmhouse. The shutters were open and he heard voices and some laughter outside. When he looked down, he saw Gerstl at his easel in the garden in front of a canvas. He then followed Gerstl's gaze towards his subject and saw Mathilde, partly immersed amidst the foliage but apparently completely naked.'

The shocked look on my face must have told its own story, as Zemlinsky went on, 'Yes, Herr Doktor, I'm sure you can imagine the scenes that followed. After Mathilde made Gerstl return to his room at the Hoisin, there was a furious row between her and Schönberg. Mathilde told him that her affair with Gerstl had been going on for some time. He begged her to stay but she said she had made up her mind. Schönberg was in a state of disbelief. All he could say was that it was impossible that his wife would ever betray or lie to him, so therefore he could no longer recognise her as his wife. By the time the others had returned from Gmunden, Mathilde had shut herself in the bedroom. Schönberg went to sleep in the children's' room but during the night he got up, unable to sleep, and discovered that the bedroom was empty and Mathilde had gone.'

'The children awoke and became upset. When Schönberg tried to comfort them, saying that their mother would be back soon, Trudi replied 'No, I saw her kissing the young man. She's never coming back'. Leaving my mother Clara to look after the children, Schönberg roused Krüger from the neighbouring farmhouse, calling to him that Mathilde had fled with Gerstl and that he was going to Gmunden to look for her. Krüger quickly threw some clothes on and together they went on foot into Gmunden, which took over an hour. They asked in every inn and hotel but without success. Later I found out from Mathilde that they stayed overnight in one of the hotels for the night as they had missed the last train to Vienna but had instructed the concierge not to divulge their presence to anybody. Reluctantly Schönberg and Krüger returned to Traunstein just before dawn. Krüger told me that by this time Schönberg was despairing and on the way back he suddenly stopped still and began to bang his head against a tree, as if he wanted to crush his own thoughts.'

Zemlinsky's story was interrupted by the waiter draining the last of the wine bottle into our glasses and taking away our plates.

'Would you like the dessert menu, *Meine Herren*?' he enquired. Zemlinsky looked over to me.

'I'll be happy with a Schwarzer and a small cognac,' he answered.

'That would be perfect for me, too, thank you,' I agreed. As soon as the waiter had left, Zemlinsky lit another cigar and relaxing back into his chair and drawing a deep breath, blew a small cloud of perfumed smoke into the air. The waiter soon returned with our glasses.

‘There is little more pleasing to the eye than the colour of a good cognac, don’t you agree, Herr Doktor?’ said Zemlinsky, holding the crystal brandy glass against the light of the flickering candle.

I nodded and smiled, offering another toast. ‘Prost!’

‘Prost!’ he repeated

‘Did Mathilde come to see you again?’ I asked, anxious that the story wasn’t lost.

‘She telephoned the next day and said she was staying in a pension in Nussdorf and asked if I had heard from Schönberg. When I said he and the children were back at home, she made me promise not to divulge where she was. Her voice was quiet and subdued; she asked if I would meet her in Nussdorf when Gerstl went to visit his mother later that day. The pension was in the main square in the village and belonged to a friend of the Gerstl family, so there were few questions asked. We met in a small cafe nearby. She looked more distressed if anything than the previous day, her suffering etched into her face; she said she had been unwell and it was obvious she had been crying. She was desperate to know about the children. She said how much she loved them and couldn’t bear the thought that she might never see them again. She knew that she was probably making a terrible mistake but there was nothing she could do to put it right and it was now all too late. The pain she was feeling was her punishment. Although she loved Gerstl, she could not live without her family. She knew Arnold would never forgive her but asked me to take him a letter. If he wants to know where she was staying, she said, just tell him that she was with good people and has a comfortable room. And tell him to kiss the children for her and ask mother to watch over them.’

‘When I returned to the Liechtensteinstrasse and delivered Mathilde’s letter to Schönberg, I was surprised to find him less agitated and sounding more positive. He had checked with the records at the police station and discovered that Mathilde had registered a change of address, as required by local law, at Nussdorferplatz 5. At least that saved me the problem of whether to betray Mathilde’s trust. It seemed quite strange to me that Schönberg asked very little about my meeting with her but, frankly, I had many other things to think about and I decided not to get any more involved. It wasn't until a couple of days later that I knocked on the door of their apartment. After a brief pause, Schönberg opened it a fraction to check who was there. 'Please keep this between us,' he whispered – his voice sounding as if it belonged to someone else – 'Mathilde is here. We are staying together for the sake of the children.' I wondered to myself how long this would last.'

Liechtensteinstrasse 70

September 1st

Richard,

I know how much pain I have caused you and I don't expect you to understand. This is the hardest decision I have ever had to make and there was no easy way out. I meant everything I told you and in a different life I would have wanted to be with you forever. But I have also to live with myself and put others first. I love Arnold and my family and I cannot cause them so much suffering. I have already hurt them enough. Please, for my sake if you love me, do not try to contact me.

Mathilde

27

As we were the almost last people in the restaurant, I suggested we move to the more comfortable lounge. We sat in the soft, low chairs in front of the last embers of the fire, while the waiter brought over our coffee and remaining brandy. Zemlinsky was looking tired and I prevented him from ordering a second cognac. I knew that if I didn't encourage him to complete his story then, it was unlikely that there would be another opportunity.

'Within a few days,' he continued, 'things began to return to normal and Schönberg contacted his students to resume lessons. Berg had just returned to Vienna after spending the summer in Villach. He was completely unaware of anything that had happened until Schönberg asked if he would take away Gerstl's portraits of him and Mathilde and keep them in his apartment until some other solution could be found. Berg went to see Gerstl in the Nussdorferstrasse, and discovered that Gerstl, in his brother's absence, had turned his bedroom into a temporary studio. Lefler had asked him to give up his Academy studio above Café Sperl. He had been working on some small paintings, the interior of the family apartment, a portrait of his mother and the view from the small Wintergarten onto the street below. However a large recently-completed canvas had obviously shocked the normally cool and cultivated Berg; an explicit full-length naked self-portrait. I'm assuming, Herr Doktor, that he was referring to the painting in your exhibition.'

'I'm sure you're right', I agreed. 'It's one of the few paintings that is signed and dated. The inscription says 12th September 1908. His brother maintains it was his last painting although there are a few rather haunting self-portraits drawings dated later in the month.'

'Actually I doubt his brother is correct about that. A short time later Gerstl found a new studio in the Liechtensteinstrasse just a few hundred metres from the apartment building where Schönberg and I lived.'

'That must have been just a few weeks before he committed suicide there', I added.

'Indeed. He and Berg had become quite close friends and around that time, Berg's sister Smaragda had tried to kill herself by putting her head in a gas oven. Gerstl's portrait of her was an engagement present but the marriage had lasted less than a year. Berg was deeply upset and he went to talk to Gerstl about his sister, as the two of them had got on well. Gerstl's new studio was on the top floor with a large skylight which looked out over the back of the Berggasse, including Freud's consulting rooms. Ironically Berg had met Freud during that summer when he had suffered a severe asthma attack in Villach and Freud, who happened to be on holiday there, treated him. Berg is a good fellow, Herr Doktor, but has always been a something of a hypochondriac.'

'So Berg visited Gerstl in his new studio?'

'That's right. Afterwards he came straight to see me because what he saw gave him cause for concern and he wanted some confidential advice. The studio was full of paintings, as not only had Gerstl cleared his home and his Academy studios but had also transported the larger canvasses back from Gmunden. It was a large painting on the easel though which took his attention; presumably the untitled female nude in your exhibition where the model is seated in front of the studio mirror. Although the sitter's facial features were still quite vague, Berg was immediately convinced it was Mathilde. Seeing it now, I am quite certain he was right. It is a rather lovely and tender painting.'

I took a slow sip of my cognac, taking in the full meaning of what Zemlinsky was saying.

'You're suggesting, Herr von Zemlinsky, that your sister was seeing Gerstl again and still modeling for him?'

'Exactly, Herr Doktor; I have to admit that I was not entirely surprised. Mathilde had certainly appeared somewhat happier. I thought that perhaps she and Schönberg had patched things up but with Schönberg busy teaching and with an important upcoming concert, I had noticed that Mathilde was keeping slightly different hours, returning home late. Berg didn't know what to do. He was very loyal to Schönberg, revered him almost but he didn't want to get involved, especially as he had no firm evidence. Not only that but Schönberg had asked Berg to take charge of the arrangements of the Musikverein concert scheduled for November 4th, featuring works by Schönberg's students, including Berg's own piano sonata to be played by Irene Bien and a new work by Webern, who was also conducting. Berg had been discharged with the task of organising the publicity, posters, invitations and tickets. This gave him another diplomatic problem, as, in normal circumstances, Gerstl would have received an automatic invite.'

'Did Berg reveal his suspicions to Schönberg then?' I asked.

'No, we thought it was better not to get involved. However, Berg decided to confide in Webern, as he was such a key part of the upcoming event. That proved to have disastrous consequences. Webern was always completely dependent on Schönberg and constantly sought his approval in his music, as well as personal affairs. Following the incident that summer over their settings of the George poems, he was anxious to repair their rather strained relationship. There was also a degree of rivalry between Webern and Berg over their closeness to Schönberg, who was virtually a father to them both. Although both were Catholics, in their character, as in their music, they were very different; Berg the romantic, Webern the ascetic. Berg was a liberal and open-minded young man while Webern was always deeply moralistic. He strongly disapproved of Mathilde's infidelity and there was little love lost between them.'

Zemlinsky paused to light another cigar.

'Without saying anything to me or Berg, Webern decided to tell Schönberg. This time Schönberg's anger was more cold and calculating, and instead of confronting Mathilde and being faced with her denial, he and Webern plotted to catch her out. With the Musikverein concert only a few days away, Schönberg was also worried about the rumours which might follow if both his wife and Gerstl were absent. The next time Webern came purportedly to discuss the performance, they asked Irene Bien to follow Mathilde when she went out. Unaware, she walked the short distance down the Liechtensteinstrasse straight to Gerstl's studio. Once Mathilde returned to the apartment, Schönberg told her he knew everything and gave her an ultimatum; either she never saw Gerstl again or he would make sure she never saw her children again. She had to choose. The children were distraught, in floods of tears, begging her to stay. Not knowing what to do, Mathilde fled in tears and knocked on our apartment door. Ida managed to calm her down and she told us what had happened. Gerstl, she said, had asked her to divorce Schönberg and marry him but for the sake of the children she already knew in her heart that she would have to sacrifice her own happiness.'

Zemlinsky was looking tired. I glanced at my watch and saw it was approaching midnight. 'If you'll forgive me, Herr Doktor, it's getting late and it has been a long day,' he said. 'The rest, I think you have worked out for yourself. From that time onwards, my sister was a broken woman. The following day, Schönberg dispatched Webern to Gerstl's studio bearing a note written by Mathilde under Schönberg's instruction, as well as to make clear that if he attempted to attend the forthcoming concert or any other future event, he would be asked to leave or be ejected.'

'How did you learn about Gerstl's death? I asked.

'Late in the evening after the Musikverein concert, which had been surprisingly well received, Gerstl's mother contacted Berg to say she was worried about him as he had not returned home, believing he had attended the performance. She added that he had seemed distressed and withdrawn in the last couple of days. When Berg told her that he had not attended the concert, Frau Gerstl sent the family maid to her son's studio who discovered the gruesome scene. As you know, Herr Doktor, Gerstl had hung himself naked in front of his studio mirror and stabbed himself in the chest. Because it was so late in the night, we were only informed the next day by Gerstl's brother. Mathilde became hysterical, broke down, sobbing uncontrollably. She stayed with us for a few days until she began to recover. She decided it would be too much to bear to attend the funeral and she didn't want to make it any more difficult for Gerstl's family.' Zemlinsky lapsed into a reflective silence, looking tired.

'You have been more than obliging, Herr von Zemlinsky, but just one last question if I might. How did Schönberg react?'

'Schönberg was deeply shocked but his first thought was about any negative consequences or scandal. As I have said to you, Herr Doktor, Schönberg and I were very close at that time but in the aftermath there was an inevitable cooling of the relationship for a period of time. Nothing could ever be quite the same again. The strained situation combined with the distressing associations made life in the Liechtensteinstrasse nigh on impossible. The next year Schönberg, generously funded by Mahler, moved to an apartment in Hietzing, which was lighter and more spacious. There he had room for a studio and started painting again. Mathilde had largely withdrawn from company and become a virtual recluse. But every year on November 4th, as long as she was in Vienna, Mathilde religiously visited Gerstl's grave to place red roses there.'

28

I caught the late morning train from the Südbahnhof. Until we reached Semmering, most compartments were quite crowded. So I stood outside in the corridor, looking at the scenery. It was rather a dreary winter landscape: the Danube with its cover of ice looked stagnant, endless brown-grey fields with occasional patches of snow, and the vast grey sky looking just as hard as the soil.

Once we passed through Semmering, the train became very quiet and I soon found an empty compartment. We climbed higher where it turned into a perfect winter's day with glorious sunshine and a fine snow cap on the tops of the wooded, rocky mountains. The Rax and the Schneeberg looked indescribably lovely in their infinite purity; all this magnificence, ever fresh and ever beautiful. Likely it was still raining in Vienna while up here I had the windows open. In the ditches below there were a few patches of fog, lit so dazzlingly by the sun that I could hardly look at them.

Once we started to descend, the fog increased, and it soon became cold and dull again. I eventually made my way down the train to the dining car, where there were barely half a dozen people and ordered lunch: veal with rice and spinach, a glass of Riesling, and for dessert, a sweet gorgonzola with butter, followed by black coffee.

After lunch, half dozing alone in my compartment, I started to ponder yet again the enigma that was Richard Gerstl. On the one hand, his uncompromising paintings, created in almost total artistic isolation, revealed a quite extraordinary self-belief and confidence with no care for what others might think. On the other hand, he had been nervous, neurotic even, about anyone seeing them, let alone exhibiting them. It was hard to imagine that even those in his immediate circle of musicians and writers, or fellow students like Hammer or teachers like Lefler, could have been able to encourage or even understand him. There must have been many times when he wondered if what he was doing had any value or purpose at all.

Yet no artist before him had made the physical substance of paint the true subject of a painting to the same degree, virtually obliterating the image with paint in the way he had in his Traunsee group portraits. And, as far as I am aware, no artist since Dürer over four hundred years previously had made a full-frontal nude male self-portrait. This painting, dated just two days before his twenty-fifth birthday and almost certainly his last completed canvas, seemed to me to somehow hold the key to the reason why Gerstl had taken his own life, even if its message continued to perplex and elude me, no matter how long I stared at it.

In its painful sincerity and typically ruthless directness, it was a cruel physical and psychological self-examination: his surgical gaze expressing his inner turmoil and isolation in the wake of Mathilde returning to Schönberg. The full exposure of his body was not aggressive or sexual in any way. His almost skeletal figure was built up from furiously agitated brushstrokes; his tall, rake-thin, white body standing out against the turquoise, dark blue and light green swirls of the wall behind him. A pulsating cobalt blue line defined the right side of his body and smears of pink and violet were scumbled into the grey-white flesh. His left hand was held out, as though making an offering of something to someone. Was it a cry for help, a statement of defiance or an admission of remorse? Certainly it was a brutal examination of his fate as an artist – and that was why I had eventually decided to give the exhibition an ambiguous title 'An Artist's Destiny'. But above all, it seemed to me to be a painting about the act of painting itself. Did he take his own life because he had lost his faith in the redemptive power of art, and its ability to ward off his increasing isolation and growing darkness inside himself?

Since so few of his paintings were dated, I had begun to put together a catalogue of his works in chronological order in an attempt to follow his stylistic development. I was aware that there were other paintings which were not in the possession of his family. The most obvious missing works were the portrait of Alban Berg's sister, Smaragda, still likely in the family's possession and the individual portraits of the Schönbergs painted in their Liechtensteinstrasse apartment. Zemlinsky had suggested that Schönberg had given these to Berg for safe-keeping, either temporarily or permanently I did not know. Over the course of the years since the exhibition, I had written on several occasions to Schönberg in Berlin but received no reply. Finally I decided to write to Berg directly but again no reply was forthcoming. As Zemlinsky had said, his loyalty to Schönberg was unequivocal. Undeterred, I had written again to him at his house near Villach in Carinthia on the shores of the Wörthersee, where I understood he now spent most of his time. Just a few weeks later I was shocked to hear of Berg's sudden death after a short illness on Christmas Eve 1935 and resigned myself to that being the end of my enquiry. A couple of months later therefore, I was taken aback when I received a letter from his sister Smaragda, inviting me to visit the lakeside house, named the Waldhaus, where she was helping to sort out her late brother's affairs.

The train pushed on towards Klagenfurt, where dark forests appeared on the horizon, which closer up became purple brown strips of woodland with bare leafless trees. New valleys then emerged, the mountains receding till at last the immense plain spread out before us with its towns and villages; beneath a pale blue sky the vast frosty meadows were almost white. At Klagenfurt I changed for Velden from where it was a short but slow journey following the lakeshore. Towards the western edge, which extended far into the mountains, I could see an idyllic small village with a church and a monastery. My eyes roamed across some fields and a forest full of winter colours surrounding the long heavily-frozen lake.

Finally from Velden it was a short cab ride to the Bergs' home. It was soon apparent that the Waldhaus was appropriately named: the road from Auen dipped through dense woodland towards the shore, narrowing all the time. Isolated from its neighbours, the house was set in its own grounds, almost hidden by vines and oak trees, only birdsong breaking the silence, a haven of peace and solitude.

29

Smaragda Berg's portrait hung in the dining room. It wasn't at all what I had been anticipating – a symphony of yellow, gold and white, broken only by the sultry dark looks and pale ivory skin of the model.

'You would never recognise me now, Doktor Nirenstein, would you?' she asked, as if reading my thoughts. Her soft dark voice still betrayed a provocative sensuality. 'I was regarded by many as a great beauty.'

'If you will allow me to say so, Frau Berg, I can easily understand why,' I replied. We were sat in the adjoining drawing room which opened out onto a small veranda. The winter sunlight through the trees threw a dappled light into the room.

'Your name, Frau Berg', I remarked, 'It's very unusual.'

'Yes,' she replied smiling, 'everyone asks. You probably won't be surprised, Herr Doktor, to learn that it was taken from one of Wagner's *Lieder*. She sang softly:

' *Hochgewölbte Blätterkronen,*
Baldachine von Smaragd,
Kinder ihr aus fernen Zonen,
Saget mir, warum ihr klagt?'

'Of course, the Wesendonck *Lieder*, I observed.

While she poured us both coffee, Smaragda began to reminisce about her brother and their early years in Vienna.

'When my wealthy Aunt Julie died, she left everything to Mother. Father had passed away a few years earlier and we were struggling to make ends meet. Alban hadn't been well, not unusually as he was asthmatic and easily prone to maladies but, much against Mother's wishes, he decided to resign from his post as a civil servant and devote himself full-time to his composition studies with Schönberg. In fact, I was the one who had originally seen an advertisement for Schönberg's classes in the *Neue Musikalische Presse* and told my older brother Charly to take along a few of Alban's songs to show him without Alban knowing. We had been brought up with music in the house, as well as a strong interest in art and the theatre. Our governess taught us both to play piano and Alban and I used to like to play duets. From the age of fifteen he began composing his own songs and setting poems to music. Often in the evenings I would sing for friends and family while Alban accompanied me on piano. In those days, we were very close and I suppose I somewhat idolised him. But while Schönberg quickly became a father-figure for him, and along with Kraus, a moral compass in his art and his life, Alban passionately loved Mahler's music more than anything.'

'I am certainly no expert,' I admitted, 'but your brother's music has always reminded me more of Mahler than Schönberg. Mahler's early death must have affected him deeply.'

'Sadly it was just a couple of weeks after Alban and Helene were married that he passed away. From that point on, Alban seemed to try to keep Mahler's memory alive by forging a strong bond with Alma Mahler, who had appointed herself as the keeper of the flame, even though they had been separated for some time. His main ambition was to sustain the Mahler ethos and as a result the audience he cared most about was Mahler's too – and first and foremost, that meant one person, Alma. He also strongly encouraged Helene in cultivating a close relationship with her and modeling herself on Alban's idealised image of her as Mahler's muse. He dedicated his first opera *Wozzeck* to Alma; in return, she gave Alban her late-husband's original manuscript of his favourite Ninth Symphony. To him, as well as many others in Vienna, Alma represented the overwhelming connection between sensuality and art, the erotic and the aesthetic, the ultimate muse, who had dominated and conquered the greatest male artists of the age, all of whom had been obsessed with her and wanted to possess her: Klimt, Zemlinsky, Mahler, Kokoschka, Gropius, Werfel, to name only a few. When Alban passed away, he was working on his second opera, *Lulu*. While I have been sorting through his things here, I have been studying the draft, which has uncanny echoes of *Tristan*, his favourite opera. I suspect that one day it may be seen as my brother's greatest work. But as you may be aware, although the symphony was performed last year not long before Alban passed away, the opera itself was not quite finished.'

'How long had your brother been working on it?' I asked.

'All in all, a very long time. Alban had admired Wedekind since his youth and when I was about eighteen or nineteen, Kraus staged a private performance of *Pandora's Box* in Vienna for an invited audience. It was banned from public stages so he hired the tiny Trianon Theatre in the Nestroyhof. Tilly Newes, Wedekind's wife, played Lulu, Wedekind himself played Jack the Ripper and even Kraus took a minor role. Alban and I went together. Everybody was there and the small auditorium was bursting at the seams. Later Richard – Gerstl, I mean – told me he had also been present though at that time I didn't know him. But it took Alban over twenty years to find a way to begin to set Wedekind's drama to music, and the work itself took him another ten.'

'Do you know why it took him so many years?' I asked.

'My brother was always a perfectionist. There is layer upon layer of meaning in his works and he was never satisfied until everything was absolutely right. Then last year, just as the opera was nearing completion, he set it aside for a few months in order to work on the *Violin Concerto* which violinist Leo Krasner had commissioned him to write. It became his requiem for Manon Gropius, Alma's daughter, who passed away last Easter. It turned out to be his last completed composition, and ironically, his own requiem as well.'

'Manon's death must have been traumatic for all those close to her,' I observed. 'She was so very young.'

'Just eighteen, Herr Doktor. Mutzi – that's how we all knew her – was indescribably beautiful. Alban and Helene loved her as if she was their own daughter and Helene keeps her framed photograph by her bed. Alban dedicated the concerto 'To the Memory of an Angel'. He worked on it at a hectic pace by his own standards and completed it last August. Due to its complexity it took Krasner some time to work out how to play it and he was eventually obliged to consult Schönberg's old friend Oskar Adler for advice. The result was that Alban lost precious time on *Lulu* but, despite the pain from the abscess on his leg which ultimately led to his fatal blood poisoning, he was soon working on it again every day, trying to get it completed. He had already begun discussions about a premiere in Prague although he really wanted it to be at the Staatsoper.'

'Why do you think the subject meant so much to him?' I asked.

'My brother's music was his way of working out his own thoughts and feelings. He often said there were only three things that really mattered – love, nature and music. Between us, Herr Doktor, I now strongly suspect that Alban based the character of Lulu on Alma.'

'What leads you to that conclusion, Frau Berg?' I asked

'Lulu is the central figure through whom art comes into being, and who more in Vienna symbolised the creative inspiration of the feminine than Alma? Klimt certainly thought so and his famous female portraits all have a hint of Alma about them – women as the object of a destructive male desire.'

'There certainly appeared to be something of an obsession with *femmes fatales* in the air at that time. As well as Klimt and Wedekind, you only have to think about Strauss' *Salome* or *Elektra*,' I observed.

'Spending a lot of time in the Café Central with Kraus and his circle, I was unable to avoid the heated debates concerning the relationship between the sexes. The role of women in society had become the controversial talking point of the day amongst writers, artists, critics, and social commentators in the coffeehouses and in the press. Amongst men naturally, I mean,' she added.

I smiled. 'Was it the publication of Weininger's book that started it?' I asked.

'I was very young, Herr Doktor, less aware than I am now. I would say that Weininger was probably more symptomatic than the cause but he summed up what many men thought: that woman was nothing but man's expression and a projection of his own fantasies and desires. I would say now that man's self-hatred caused a hatred for women which had to be killed.'

'Kokoschka's drama, of course, *Murderer, Hope of Women* – Love was murder. Do you know it?' I asked her.

'I actually remember going to the premiere at the Kunstschau with my good friend Elk Miethke, the wife of the gallery owner. I found it rather unpleasant and disturbing but in those days the relationship between men and women was so often portrayed as a violent conflict or battle. I suppose looking back it was a period when so much in society was changing. Women were making slow progress with more educational opportunities and becoming increasingly involved with political and social causes. People were talking about the 'New Woman': independent, educated and more sexually liberated with a valuable role to play in society rather than just in the home. Traditionally women had been more closely linked with irrationality, nature, and body, because they were often seen as driven by out-of-control physical urges, and men were conversely assigned to the side of reason, discourse, culture and intellect. Hysteria had come to stand for the feminine unconscious gone wild.'

'Freud's *Studies in Hysteria* was a typical example, I suppose,' I remarked. 'His patients were almost exclusively female.'

'Well, yes. Freud did actually complain that Weininger had stolen his ideas! Western culture had been created by males. Women had advanced or impeded cultural developments solely by inspiring or inhibiting male efforts; their role in society was exclusively erotic and aesthetic. The rise of women appeared a threat to the established male moral order.'

'May I ask you, Frau Berg, as one of the few females readily accepted in those circles, how you felt surrounded by those views?'

'I had two advantages, Herr Doktor. Firstly, I was rather rebellious in my youth and lived a very Bohemian lifestyle. Secondly, my attraction to other women was a well-known secret within that circle and the curious reverse of their views was that since male and female were polar opposites, the lesbian was regarded as the highest form of woman, the one most like men, because she transcended her sexuality and attraction to men.'

'Did you ever discuss these ideas with Gerstl?' I enquired.

'Yes, sometimes. Although Richard was at first rather shy and quiet, beneath that he held strong views. He saw an inner contradiction in the artistic ideas espoused by the so-called radicals and their old-fashioned conservative moral code, and he was sympathetic to my view that women were treated as an inferior species. As usual with Richard, he related it to art and Klimt was always the major focus of his criticism; he particularly disliked the way Klimt painted his female models as objects. You can see in my portrait, Herr Doktor, how Richard depicted his subjects in a very different way.'

'Certainly there is none of Klimt's sense of neurosis,' I replied, 'I am still struck in your painting by its patterned, almost decorative Klimt-like quality, almost as if Gerstl was mimicking him.'

'As you say, the interior has a very strong geometric design. When Alban brought Richard to the family house in Hietzing, he seemed to have a very clear idea of how he wanted to set the painting up. What appeared to concern him most of all was the composition. Since it was in reality a commissioned portrait, I must admit that I was slightly surprised that he made no attempt to consult Alban or me.'

'How did the painting come about?'

'Schönberg suggested the idea to my brother. Richard had recently completed Schönberg's portrait, as well as Mathilde's, and was looking for more sitters. Alban was impressed by what he had seen – the paintings hung in the Schönbergs' apartment – and he mentioned it to my fiancé Adolf Ritter von Eger, who readily agreed. It was painted at the time of my engagement and you can see I am wearing my engagement dress and ring. Alban and I knew Klimt very well – his studio was close to our villa – and I think my brother had in mind his portraits of society women, which had become highly fashionable in affluent Jewish circles.'

'Didn't you or your brother consider approaching Klimt himself for the task?'

'Alban admired Klimt's paintings but Richard wasn't the only one who didn't share that view. The Café Central was the place where we often all met in the evenings. I usually sat at Kraus' table with Loos and PA – Altenberg, that is. It was PA's second home, and he became rather infatuated with me, as he was with many women, including Helene. Klimt was also a regular there with his own circle but the two groups would often cross over. Kraus was always the dominant intellectual figure and arbiter of taste, revered by Alban, and along with Loos, he was highly critical of Klimt's paintings. Alban never quite knew whose side to take. Another problem was Klimt's notorious reputation with his models and my fiancé didn't want any gossip spreading. Poor Adolf didn't realise the irony, as he didn't understand at that time that I would have been totally safe with Klimt. But all those close to me were well aware that my attraction was to other women far more than men.'

'Were you and Gerstl already acquainted?'

'Actually I believe I probably first met Richard one evening in the Fledermaus Cabaret, which had recently opened in the Kärntnerstrasse. Do you remember it, Herr Doktor?'

'I was too young but I have heard about it, of course.'

'It was in the cellar of an apartment block on the corner of Johannesgasse. The interior was an artwork in itself, created by the Wiener Werkstätte; the entrance and bar had a black and white marble floor with walls completely covered in colourful majolica tiles, while the main auditorium was painted totally white. It soon became the place to go, and the talk of Vienna's cultural circles; its program regularly featured famous singers and dancers such as the Wiesenthal sisters and most of the well-known literary names of the day, including Friedell, Polgar and, of course, PA. My good friend, the well-known chanteuse, Marya Delvard was performing there one night soon after it opened, and Richard came along with Alban. They had originally met at Schönberg's, of course, and got on well together. They soon became good friends.'

'How long did it take Gerstl to complete your painting?' I asked.

'Probably not more than half a dozen sittings; Richard painted quickly and each sitting would last for up to a couple of hours or so. He concentrated hard and spoke little while he was working but he would sometimes take a break and then we would talk. Or he might stay a while after we had finished a sitting.'

'How was the portrait received?'

'Hardly anybody saw it. Alban liked it a great deal but Erich knew almost nothing about art. I have grown to become very fond of it but for a long time the painting's associations with my engagement and very brief marriage made it difficult for me to look at.'

'Did you see Gerstl at all once the painting was finished?'

'In the autumn, once the music season had begun, I saw him a few times at the Hofoper or the Musikverein when he would sometimes be accompanied by Mathilde Schönberg. Alban explained that Schönberg was invariably busy with his private tuition in the evenings, so he would ask Richard to take Mathilde with him to concerts.'

'Can you remember much about the events leading up to Gerstl's death?' I asked.

'That period of my life feels fairly hazy, I'm afraid, Herr Doktor. I was preoccupied with my own problems, dreading a marriage I hadn't chosen, which predictably from the very first day proved an unmitigated disaster; Erich, who was a decent man, just wasn't able to understand and we argued all day and all night. I became deeply depressed and was on the verge of a breakdown. Mother had moved from Hietzing to an apartment near the Stadtpark and I went to live with her and Alban. The only person who understood was Helene and we became very close, though Alban then started to become jealous of our intimacy. Within a few months Erich and I were separated. Mother was very upset about it and I began to spend most of my nights in the cafes and nightclubs again with my girlfriends, drinking heavily and becoming involved in a succession of meaningless affairs. Sometimes I would see Richard with Alban and Schönberg at the Löwenbräukeller, their regular haunt. But I would be with Altenberg and his coterie of actresses and singers, and from there we would move on to the Nachlicht or another club. When I got back home in the early hours, I would often annoy Alban by waking him up to tell him the story of my latest conquest.'

'As usual during the summer months we all went to the Berghof, the family estate on the Ossiachersee. Just before Alban left in early July, I recall him telling me he had visited the Kunstschau with Richard, who he said was intending to stay with Schönberg and his students on the Traunsee. I remained for a little longer in Vienna with my brother Charly, before joining Alban and Mother, as well as our eldest brother Hermann and his wife, who had come over from America. Not long after we arrived, Alban suffered a particularly severe asthma attack. Fortunately a doctor was quickly located staying at a nearby hotel in Annenheim, who we soon realised was the famous Dr. Sigmund Freud on holiday from Vienna. Also staying at the hotel for the summer was a group of attractive young women from Vienna. One of them developed a crush on Alban while I fell in love with another, and over the next few weeks we spent quite a lot of time together.'

'Did you hear any news from the Traunsee?' I enquired.

'If Alban did, he certainly didn't tell me. But I doubt it, as he was still recuperating and doing very little. I don't think he was even writing very much to Helene, who had gone with her parents to stay near Meran in the South Tyrol for the summer. Then towards the end of August, Alban went to Venice for a few days at the invitation of friends, mainly to visit the house where Wagner had died. Once he returned, he decided to stay on at the Berghof after the rest of the family had gone home. He always much preferred the Berghof out-of-season when most of the tourists had left the lake. Since I had no need or desire to go back to Vienna, I decided to stay on with him. The weather however quickly turned for the worse with howling storms and incessant heavy rain. So a week later we reluctantly set off back to Vienna where there was still some late summer sun. Alban was soon very busy, dealing with the administration of the property the family now owned and resuming his lessons with Schönberg, who had asked him to help organise a concert by his students scheduled for early November in the Musikverein. Vienna can be a lonely place and I felt very isolated, spending most of the time at home or just sitting and walking for hours alone in the nearby Stadtpark. Eventually I suffered a crisis which led to a complete nervous breakdown, and ultimately I made an attempt to take my own life. I suppose in truth it was a cry for help. I was filled with anxiety and despair and didn't know who to turn my guilt and anger against, so I directed it against myself and against life.'

'I am so sorry, Frau Berg,' I said. 'I had no intention of bringing those memories back for you. There really is no need for you to continue if it's too difficult.'

'There is no need to be concerned, Herr Doktor, it was all a long time ago,' she replied quietly. The sun had dipped behind the trees and the room had become quite gloomy. 'I didn't know until much later about what happened to Richard. Alban decided it would be too much for me to deal with and in any case it became clear when I eventually found out that the whole incident had been covered up as if it had never happened. I didn't hear Richard's name mentioned again for a very long time.'

30

'Let me put some more wood on the fire, Herr Doktor,' Smaragda said. As it spluttered and flickered back into life, she switched on a couple of lamps, before sitting back down to continue her story.

'As soon as I began to recover, I knew that the first thing I had to do was to escape Vienna,' she went on. 'I moved to Munich and settled in Schwabing. Writers, artists, performers and musicians regularly congregated in the many smoke-filled bohemian cafes there. I fell madly in love with the Spanish dancer Anna Sunen and I was able to live my life as I pleased without being judged by others. I had come across the composer Thomas von Hartmann, a pupil of Felix Mottl, director of the Munich Opera House and himself a former pupil of Wagner. With his wife Olga, he also lived in Schwabing in the Ainmillerstrasse, where his best friend and neighbour was Wassily Kandinsky.'

'Kandinsky's paintings of that period have always been particular favourites of mine,' I interrupted, 'especially those landscapes of Murnau with the village and the church tower. I'm aware, of course, that he and Schönberg got to know each other around that time. Was your brother acquainted with Kandinsky too?'

'Yes, it came about through Schönberg,' Smaragda replied. 'While I was in Munich, there was a performance of Schönberg's Three Piano Pieces and Second String Quartet. Von Hartmann had written the musical sketch for Kandinsky's theatre project *Der Gelbe Klang* which bore uncanny similarities to Schönberg's music dramas. Von Hartmann brought Kandinsky along with several other Blaue Reiter artist friends such as Marc and Jawlensky. Kandinsky instinctively recognised a kindred spirit in Schönberg; both were tearing up all the established rules and driving their art in completely new directions with little critical or public understanding. I put him in touch with Schönberg and a short time later Schönberg came to stay with Zemlinsky on the Starnberger See. Zemlinsky had been invited to conduct at the Künstlertheater in Munich for the summer. They rented a house across the lake from the villa in Murnau which Kandinsky's wife Gabriele Münter owned, and where they painted during the summer months. The Kandinskys were often joined by Jawlensky and his wife, so it soon became known as the Russian House. That was Kandinsky's and Schönberg's first meeting and from then on, they corresponded frequently. Quite independently, Kandinsky was just completing his book '*On the Spiritual in Art*' at the same time as Schönberg's '*Theory of Harmony*' was being published, which was I suppose in many ways its musical equivalent. My brother had been heavily involved in the editing and the compiling of Schönberg's book, as well as being the contact point with the publishers in Munich. As a result Kandinsky used the same publishers for his Blaue Reiter Almanach and invited Alban to contribute one of his scores. If you wish, Herr Doktor, I can show you my brother's study where he kept his treasured copies of those books?'

She led me to a small room on the side of the house; it contained a simple writing desk with a window looking out onto the woods, a library and a piano on which stood a framed portrait of Mahler. 'It is exactly as it was on the day he died. Helene wants to keep it this way.'

'How long were you in Munich?' I asked.

'About three years. My relationship with Anna had ended and I had met May Keller, with whom I have shared my life for the last twenty years. Schönberg had left Vienna to teach at the Stern Conservatory in Berlin and wrote to me inviting me to the rehearsals for his new work *Pierrot Lunaire*. The Schönbergs were living in the top storey of a villa in Zehlendorf out towards the Wannsee on the remote fringes of the city. The woods with their pines and birches grew right into the gardens of the houses. The garden had a large pond, next to which stood a lovely summer house. It was called the Villa Lepcke and belonged to the wealthy Albertine Zehme, who had commissioned Schönberg's new song cycle. It was a haven of tranquility and there was plenty of room not only for the family but visiting guests and musicians as well. Seeing Mathilde again, I soon realised she was a shadow of the woman I had last seen in Vienna. Her mother's recent death appeared to have taken a further toll; she rarely left the house and sat most of the time in silence like an invalid, looking twenty years older. May and I immediately fell in love with Berlin as it was so full of life and energy. We soon found a small attic apartment in Charlottenburg and I resumed my voice and piano lessons. One of my first students was a young Frida Leider, who at the time was working in a bank.'

'I saw her sing *Isolde* at Bayreuth a few years ago,' I replied. 'She has such an extraordinarily pure and tender voice.'

'Yes, Herr Doktor, she is now probably the greatest Wagnerian soprano of our generation. Schönberg then asked me if I would help out with his rehearsals for the forthcoming concerts, so we decided to stay permanently. Schönberg himself was not a particularly accomplished pianist and *Pierrot* was scheduled to tour to several venues across Europe. There was also the premiere of his epic cantata *Gurrelieder* in Vienna to rehearse. At very short notice, following a recital he had heard her give in Berlin, he asked the Polish soprano Marya Freund to take the main role. He was also very conscious that the public performances of the new music had become increasingly scandalous. They soon culminated in a concert back in Vienna, which I'm sure you are of aware of, Herr Doktor.'

'The notorious concert at the Musikverein, I presume you mean? Were you present?'

'I went from Berlin with Marya, who was supposed to be performing Mahler's *Kindertotenlieder*, the final work on the program. However, it didn't get that far. From the very beginning, which was the premiere of Webern's *Six Pieces for Orchestra*, there were catcalls and laughter. Once it reached Schönberg's *Chamber Concerto*, the audience had lost patience and was almost out of control. Alban's *Altenberg Lieder* proved the final straw. Schönberg, who was conducting, banged on the podium, demanding quiet, and even threatened to call the police. But it was to no avail. By the time Marya took the stage, the hall was in total chaos. Many were insulted that Mahler's music had been included in such a program. The lights were switched on. When it was announced that the rest of the concert was cancelled, pandemonium broke out. Fighting began among the audience while the musicians fled the stage. The auditorium then went dark while the police finally arrived to clear the hall.'

'Why do you think that the reaction was so hostile?' I asked.

'There was a strong feeling that the new music was threatening the established social order; it sounded like it was on the verge of breakdown, some portent of chaos and anarchy.'

'Which, of course,' I concluded for her, 'engulfed Europe only a year later.'

31

Smaragda pointed to some photographs hanging in the study, including one of her brother in uniform. 'Did you serve during the war, Herr Doktor?' she asked.

'Yes, although it seems like another lifetime now. I fought on the Eastern Front in Russia and then in the South Tyrol against the Italians. I was too young to question it. And your brother?' I asked.

'When he was called up, Alban was sent to a training camp but he was soon declared unfit for service due to his chronic asthma. So he worked for most of the war in Vienna as an official in the War Ministry, where he was able to live in his own apartment and continue his life in Vienna's musical circles. It was during this period that he began work on *Wozzeck*, his first opera, which of course depicts the daily life of a lowly soldier. Schönberg and Webern had joined the army too; initially they were all fiercely patriotic, and believed that they were fighting for a great, sublime cause: the preservation of the Austrian Empire and civilisation against the forces of capitalism and a new barbaric mechanisation. The idea took root that science had failed and there was a need for a spiritual rebirth and that the war would be the forecasted apocalypse which would purge the world of evil.'

'Certainly Kandinskys early paintings are full of images of the apocalypse,' I remarked. 'Did everyone in those circles feel that way about the war?'

'The only one who vehemently disagreed was Kraus, who recognised the blind stupidity and hypocrisy of it all from the beginning,' Smaragda replied. 'Editions of *Die Fackel* were frequently censored or banned; Alban revered Kraus; and as you can see there on the shelf, he had every copy of *Die Fackel* carefully bound. But as the war dragged on, others slowly came round to Kraus' way of thinking. With the growing realisation of the horrors of the war, many people started to look for more esoteric solutions, and the artist was seen as a spiritual leader.'

'For Kandinsky art was a religion,' I said. 'He saw both colour and music as gateways to the soul and a higher realm, and often talked about making the invisible visible. He claimed that colours could be heard and sounds could be seen by those with a higher perception. For him it was proof that a world existed beyond the physical world – a fourth dimension located in space not time.'

'I well remember the Kandinskys' evenings in their Ainmillerstrasse apartment,' Smargada replied. 'They would invite friends to take part in their synaesthetic experiments. Von Hartmann would first select one of Kandinsky's watercolours and play an improvised musical version on the piano. Then they were joined by the dancer Alex Sakharoff who would dance to the music and everyone had to guess which painting he had danced.'

'What did you feel about these ideas?' I asked her.

'Well, at that time in Schwabing occult societies had become something of a fashion. What appealed to me most personally was that it was mainly women who first became involved, drawing in friends, family and assuming positions of power. Olga was a loyal follower of Helena Blavatsky. It seemed somehow to go hand in hand with the growing feminist movement. The Theosophical Society was run by a succession of women, mediums were almost all women, and often rebellious. It seemed like a challenge to the dominance of traditional male ways of thinking and authority from a female and spiritual perspective, which had become linked.'

I had already noticed books on Berg's shelves by Blavatsky's fellow Theosophists Charles Leadbeater and Annie Besant. Their *Thought Forms* had attempted to translate emotions into colour and form some years ahead of Kandinsky. I asked Smaragda if Schönberg and her brother had shared Kandinsky's fascination with mysticism and the occult.

'I didn't really think about it much until later although I was aware that they both had long held a superstitious obsession about numbers.'

'Can you tell me some more about that?' I asked her.

'Well, Schönberg held a morbid fear of the number 13 and anything associated with it – he was dreading his 39th birthday – while my brother referred repeatedly to the number 23 and its multiples as his fateful number, one that played a mysterious and decisive role in his life.'

'Was there any particular reason for it?'

'I never really knew. He always said that his first asthma attack had happened on that date but it became something much more complex. He took special interest in dates, addresses, telegrams which bore that number. We are still not entirely sure if he passed away on the 24th of last December as is officially recorded or the previous night of the 23rd. He also completed several of his major compositions on that date. When Alban visited Berlin, it became clear to me that his obsession had even begun to dictate the structure of his compositions, and he and Schönberg discussed these ideas at length.'

'Unfortunately my technical knowledge of music is somewhat limited, Frau Berg,' I replied.

'I'm not sure as yet we fully understand the complexity of my brother's music, Herr Doktor. The more I study it the more I find. It is increasingly apparent to me that there are many levels of cryptic clues hidden in his compositions, all of which seem to have some autobiographical significance. After *Wozzeck* they seem to have become a vital and obsessive part of his working method but now they seem like messages from beyond the grave.'

'That sounds quite disturbing. Can you give me some examples in simpler terms?'

'His Chamber Concerto is a good example, which he dedicated to Schönberg on his 50th birthday. Although his fateful number was 23, he also interpreted the numbers separately, as 2 and 3. These numbers dictate the length, structure and proportions of his compositions. The concerto has three movements and three principal motives celebrating the three great radical friends, my brother, Schönberg and Webern. Their three names are translated into musical notes which are woven inextricably into the piece. Even the number of instruments, 15, is divisible by three as an homage to Schönberg's First Symphony. But even more significantly the adagio is divided into two sections, each comprising 120 bars, with the second 120 bars a complete reversal of the first.'

'So, to put it simply, you mean it's the same music played backwards?'

'Yes, that's right; note for note. A mirror image. Or circular, because the end takes you back to the beginning.'

'Just like Kandinsky's obsession with circles,' I added. 'A kind of eternal recurrence.'

'What's more, Herr Doktor, he split the two sections of the adagio with twelve sombre low notes on the piano.'

'Like the tolling of a midnight bell?'

'Exactly; as if for a tragic death. But, even more eerily, studying my brother's notes I have discovered that the adagio has another name embedded in it – Mathilde's. She passed away on October 22nd 1923.'

32

Outside an icy winter night had fallen and we went back to sit by the warmth of the fire, as Smaragda concluded her story.

'When war was declared Schönberg was staying in Murnau with Kandinsky. While Kandinsky made his way back to Russia, Schönberg returned to Berlin to await his military call-up. As that didn't immediately come, Alma Mahler invited him to Vienna a few months later to conduct her late husband's revised version of Beethoven's 9th symphony. She had persuaded her wealthy friend Lilly Lieser to sponsor it as a benefit concert for struggling musicians. When Frau Lieser offered Schönberg an apartment in Hietzing, he decided to move back to Vienna for good, which in truth came as something of a relief. Relations between us had become decidedly cool, especially after I told him that Mathilde was badly in need of help. May and I decided to remain in Berlin.'

'Despite Alma being caught in the middle of stormy relationships with Kokoschka and Gropius,' Smaragda continued, 'she found time to secure the Gustav Mahler Trust for Schönberg, a fund that offered support for needy composers. But a number of problems leading up to and following the benefit concert caused anxieties for both Alma and Schönberg, which resulted in a strained friendship between them. Since Alban was both Schönberg's most devoted student and a close friend of Alma's, he tried to help mend the relationship but Schönberg suspected he and Alma were plotting against him. It caused a rift between them for a period but Alban, Helene and Alma grew closer.'

'After the war began Helene spent increasing amounts of time at Haus Mahler, Alma's newly-built villa in Breitenstein near Semmering. She had designed the house around an enormous fireplace above which Kokoschka had painted a very large fresco, prophetically depicting himself burning in the fires of hell while Alma soared away towards heaven. Much to Kokoschka's annoyance, in pride of place in the house she kept the death mask she had commissioned of her late husband. Once Alma became pregnant with Manon, Gropius' daughter, she would frequently give Helene lists of food to send or bring with her; her favourite fruits in particular, apples, blueberries and cherries, but also beef, vegetables or butter, none of which were easy to obtain in wartime Vienna. Alma would have to send someone to pick her up at Semmering station after the three and a half hour train journey as she would arrive loaded down with goods. Helene was always very careful with money and made a lot of her own clothes; sometimes she would take presents for Alma and the newly-born baby, such as shawls and jackets which she had knitted herself. Whenever Helene was there, she would help out with the household duties, while Alban joined them as much as his military duties allowed. Like Alma's regular Sunday salons at her Elisabethstrasse apartment, Haus Mahler soon became a meeting place not only for a variety of musicians, artists and writers but also for spiritual philosophers and mystics of all kinds. Helene had told me that in New York, Mahler and Alma, still grieving after the tragic death of their beloved young daughter Putzi, were introduced to spiritualism by the banker and cultural philanthropist Otto Kahn, who was Chairman of the Metropolitan Opera, where Mahler was employed. Together they attended a number of séances. Since Mahler's death, Alma had increasingly immersed herself in occult readings, in particular Besant and Leadbeater's books that you noticed in Alban's library, and she had joined the Theosophical Society. But it wasn't until I moved back to Vienna that I realised that not only had Alma become fascinated with these ideas but Helene and Alban as well.'

'When did you actually return?' I asked.

'Not until the war was over. By then Berlin had turned into complete chaos. There was a general strike and the Communists and Fascists were fighting daily in the streets. It quickly became just too dangerous to stay. Part of the family inheritance from Aunt Julie had been a small summer house in Küb near Semmering, which was rarely used. So May and I managed to escape there. The house was very close to Alma's, just ten minutes from Breitenstein on the Semmeringbahn.'

I was curious to know if she had ever come across the artist Johannes Itten there. 'I believe that Itten was a frequent visitor,' I remarked. 'For a short time I studied at his private art school, then later, while I was working for Würthle's, I was responsible for the publication of a portfolio of his prints. I got to know him quite well.'

'Not at Breitenstein but I met him once or twice at Schönberg's Society for Private Musical Performances. I particularly remember an afternoon rehearsal of Schönberg's Chamber Symphony at the Musikvereinsaal. Everyone seemed to be there that day – Alban, Webern, Altenberg, Loos, Zemlinsky and Alma, who brought Itten along with her. Afterwards we all went back to Alma's nearby apartment. I must say he struck me as a rather curious character, very serious and intense, like a monk. I understood he was a close friend of Josef Hauer, who was also there that day and always claimed to have invented twelve-tone music before Schönberg. Of course Itten then left Vienna soon after to teach at the Bauhaus in Weimar where he was later joined by Kandinsky.'

'Yes, that's right,' I replied. 'Itten told me it was Alma Mahler in fact who first took Gropius to his studio in the Nussdorferstrasse to see his abstract paintings. Although he said Gropius openly admitted that he didn't understand them, Alma persuaded her husband that if he wanted to have any chance of success with the Bauhaus project, he needed to appoint him. So Gropius offered him the position as one of the first three Bauhaus Masters. His students were more like disciples and a number of them followed him from Vienna. They regarded him as a saint and soon began to dress like him, act like him and think like him. By that time he had completely shaved his head, and wore round eye glasses and an austere wine-red Bauhaus uniform of his own design.'

'I certainly recall that he shared Alma's passion for eastern mysticism,' said Smaragda. 'And Weimar seemed to have become a particular magnet for all types of strange mystics and believers of those new faiths which had sprung up throughout Europe after the war.'

'Yes, that's true. Adolf Meyer, Gropius' partner, was a committed Theosophist. Then there were others such as Rudolf Hausser, who converted a number of the Bauhaus students and persuaded them to accompany him on a pilgrimage; and most curious of all, there was the so-called 'barefoot apostle', the naturopath Gustav Nagel. He dressed like Jesus and spelled his name in lower case, because he believed in the abolition of capital letters, a precursor of the Bauhaus' own typography.'

'Was Itten a Theosophist as well?' Smaragda asked.

'No, he had become a rather zealous member of the more extreme Mazdaznan sect who were followers of Zoroaster. In common with many Eastern mystics, they believed that vegetarianism, fasting and meditation were the means to making the mind and body receptive to true reality. It was after Rabindranath Tagore's visit to Weimar that Itten organised the first Bauhaus exhibition outside Germany, which took place in Calcutta. But, unfortunately, it all ended in something of a scandal. Much to Itten's annoyance, the loan exhibits mysteriously disappeared somewhere in India and never found their way back to Germany.'

Smaragda smiled. 'Alban told me later on that Kandinsky invited Schönberg to apply for the position as Director of the Bauhaus School of Music but he refused.'

'Did he explain why?' I asked.

'Schönberg had heard rumours about anti-Semitic feelings at the Bauhaus and Alma had suggested to him that the Kandinskys shared them.'

'That surprises me. Do you think there was any truth in it?'

'I doubt it regarding the Kandinskys. But Alma loved spreading gossip and Schönberg had also become a regular visitor to Haus Mahler. By this time, the Schönbergs had left Hietzing and moved to Mödling, where rents were cheaper. They were desperately struggling for money. Food and coal were in short supply except at high prices on the black market. Schönberg was still wearing his military trousers and a coat that was far too big for him, and the children wore patched-up hand-me-downs. Their apartment was always bitterly cold and Mathilde spent most of her time in bed. She was suffering from anemia and looked as pale as a ghost. She did so little that Webern's wife used to go over there regularly to clean and take care of other household chores. When Schönberg was invited by Zemlinsky to conduct four guest concerts for the Society in Prague, he asked Alma to keep an eye on Mathilde and the children while he was away. Both Alma and Helene were firmly of the opinion that her physical sickness was mainly the symptom of a spiritual sickness. It was hard not to agree; she barely spoke and showed little interest in anything. As Schönberg stubbornly refused to recognise the seriousness of Mathilde's condition, they decided to take the opportunity to see if they could help her.'

'Do you mean professional medical help or psychoanalysis?'

'Mahler had consulted Freud before his death after Alma had left him. But Freud did himself no favours in Alma's eyes by pursuing payment after his death. But apart from that, both she and Alban were always under Kraus' influence and were, like him, deeply suspicious of Freud's theories and techniques.'

'Yes, I recall his typically witty description of psychoanalysis as 'the illness of which it pretends to be the cure'!'

'Exactly, Herr Doktor. Alma and Helene took a similar view. Haus Mahler had also become a regular meeting place for Alma's friends in the Theosophical Society and she regularly invited a spiritual healer to Breitenstein. She was convinced that the séances she had attended in America after the death of her daughter had helped her deal with her grief. Helene told me this was not entirely approved of by her fellow members, who saw any attempt to communicate with the after-life as a serious danger to all involved, but in particular to the guide and the spirits themselves.'

'I always understood that was a significant part of their belief,' I said.

'Only in certain circumstances, Helene told me. In contrast to spiritualists, according to the theosophical doctrine, an impassable chasm exists between the physical and the spiritual planes, so that those who have passed away are entirely out of reach while they wait for rebirth. Although everyone leaves behind an astral shell, it is merely a shadow containing the individual's cast-off memories and all those mundane characteristics which are unable to enter the heavenly state. It is easy for a fraudulent or inexperienced medium to mistake this for the real departed soul.'

'There are however some exceptions, specifically those whose life has been prematurely cut short,' Smaragda explained. 'They are obliged to stay within the atmosphere of the Earth for the entire remaining duration of the life they had been destined to live. Alma saw the young daughter and husband she had lost in this category. Tragic victims of accident or suicide, or even murder find themselves trapped in an in-between state on the astral plane. Because they are often deeply unhappy and full of regrets, they are more tempted to try to make contact with the life they have left behind through a medium, and more vulnerable to a medium contacting them. But in doing so, they run the risk of losing their soul forever when their allotted life term reaches its end. And a dark fate will also be in store for any medium who causes it to happen.'

'Did this not deter Frau Mahler?' I asked.

'She firmly believed that she had made contact with her late husband a number of times and she always kept his death mask close at hand during the séance. On this occasion however she arranged the séance more with Mathilde in mind, although of course she didn't tell her that. She was confident that Mathilde would have no objections, as she had claimed that since her mother Clara's death, she had appeared to her on several occasions and even spoken with her. She seemed to see nothing unusual in it. But Alma and Helene were convinced that a healer would be able to establish the root cause of Mathilde's melancholy and channel healing energies from the spirit world that would bring peace and harmony to the mind, body and spirit. They asked me to attend and I agreed, albeit slightly reluctantly.'

'You had reservations?'

'I was unsure that it would help and thought it might do more harm than good. Helene persuaded me that it was worth trying but neither of us were prepared for what actually happened.'

'Who else was present?'

'Just the four of us, as well as the medium. The view was it should be kept to a minimum as communication with the after-life would be much more likely if everyone present believed in its possibility. Any sense of scepticism in the room would weaken the chances of the likelihood of the spirits making their presence known.'

'Was it the first time you had attended a séance?'

'In Munich I had been once or twice to séances at the Hartmanns. But they were more like public events, almost verging on theatre. One evening with Kandinsky and others, Olga decided to try running a plate with an arrow on it around the German alphabet. We asked it questions, hoping it would stop on letters and spell out a message. But nothing happened of any meaning. So we decided to try in Russian, and at once it became quite exciting. A spirit spelled out her name, claiming to have lived and been buried somewhere in a small village in Siberia and asked us to pray for her. She started to tell us about her cousin still living there but at that point the message was interrupted and was lost. Kandinsky later decided to write to the local priest who replied to say that there was indeed someone by that name living in the village.'

'This was different though?' I prompted her.

'Much more private. It was very late into the evening, as there was less chance of interruption and a relaxed mind, the medium said, was much more open to supernatural possibilities. Alma had set up her study at Haus Mahler with five chairs around a table on which stood some candles. The room was in semi-darkness, lit with just one lamp but once the candles were lighted, the lamp was switched off as we took our places. The medium asked us to link hands while she closed her eyes and she started to breathe slowly and deeply. After a few minutes she invited the spirits to join the circle and asked whether there were any spirits who had a message for any of those present. There followed a long period of silence as we waited for a speaker. Alma started to become a little restless but the medium anticipated her. 'I told you it would be difficult,' she said. 'Please be patient.' A few more minutes elapsed and the medium seemed to pass into a different state of consciousness, as if in a trance or under hypnosis. She started to make odd sounds but it was impossible to make out what she was saying. It sounded like cries or odd fragments of words, which came and went, rather like a wireless having difficulty being tuned into the right station. But at last she composed herself and spoke clearly and slowly, 'Somebody here is in unbearable pain' she said. I feel a terrible loss and suffering such as I never felt before. Please, don't be frightened, I have a message for you.' Nobody spoke but I felt an increased tension in Alma's hands to my right and Mathilde's to my left, while opposite Helene had visibly paled. The room seemed to have suddenly become much colder and I shivered. Again it was quiet for a short time before the medium more hesitatingly continued. 'Music,' she said. 'I can hear a strange kind of music.' Alma couldn't restrain herself any longer. 'Gustav! My darling Putzi!' she cried out. 'I beg you, please give me a message!' But the medium had gone back into a trance-like state and was silent again. I was hoping that might be the end, as it had become more disturbing than I had ever imagined. Alma was in tears, while Helene and Mathilde looked extremely confused and distressed. But then the medium spoke again, softly now as if in a dream. 'I hear a woman's voice, not singing but calling to someone. There is a lake. It's late at night. I can see a farmhouse with a white balcony and dark wooden shutters surrounded by a forest. The woman is calling to someone, screeching wildly now, as if in pain. She is searching for something and stumbles across a fallen tree. She sits down but something is there, hidden underneath it. She reaches down. It is hard to make out what it is, the night is so black.' Mathilde had frozen, her hands rigid.

There was a silence. I looked at the medium. Her eyes were now wide open, staring straight ahead into space as if suddenly realising what she was seeing. She became extremely animated, 'Red!' she cried. 'I can see a bloody red, on her dress, her hands and her face.' But as she spoke, next to me, Mathilde collapsed unconscious onto the floor and the circle was broken.'

33

What will become of Gerstl's paintings, now gathering dust again in a Viennese warehouse? If discovered, they would certainly be destroyed as 'Jewish pornography'. So far I am finding little interest here in New York in Austrian artists. My first exhibition 'Austrian Masters', including works by Klimt, Schiele and Kokoschka, has attracted little critical response and few potential buyers. Most of the interest has come from the ever-growing number of Austrian refugees here, who hardly have enough money to survive, never mind buy paintings. In fact, the gallery has quickly become a centre and meeting place for the émigré Austrian community in New York. I have recently been invited to join the Austrian-American League, whose aim is to preserve Austrian culture and provide practical help to émigrés with visas and permits, as well as the general problems of life in a new and strange world.

There was, however, one wholly unexpected visitor, Zemlinsky's wife Louise. Remarkably she explained that they were now resident on Manhattan's Upper West Side, just a short walk across Central Park from our apartment. Louise had been a student of her husband but, as well as being a professional singer, she was a talented artist, who had originally trained at the Prague Academy and painted all her life. They had fled Vienna soon after the *Anschluss*. Once they had received an initial visit from the Gestapo, they immediately destroyed all photos and correspondence, particularly of Zemlinsky's Turkish-Muslim grandmother and Spanish-Jewish grandfather, which might betray his ethnic origins.

Their applications for visas to the United States were delayed, Frau Zemlinsky told me, as they were mistakenly informed quota numbers were full.

Instead, they managed to obtain passports to visit her family in Prague, but not before having to pay the newly-imposed Nazi 'refugee tax', amounting to one quarter of their savings. They escaped in the late summer of 1938 just weeks before *Kristallnacht*, when nearly every synagogue in Austria and Germany was destroyed, including the Sephardic Synagogue of Zemlinsky's youth, whose history had been so lovingly documented by his father Adolf.

In November their visas to travel to America were finally granted and, early in December, the Zemlinskys flew to Rotterdam before travelling on to France. They had arrived in New York just two days before Christmas when they were met by Melanie Guttmann Rice, Zemlinsky's youthful love and sister of his first wife Ida. She had moved to New York over thirty years ago to live with her husband, the artist William Clarke Rice, who had passed away ten years previously. It was the first time that Zemlinsky had seen her since they had visited Europe in the summer of 1907. Melanie took them to the Hotel Hamilton on West 73rd Street but they soon found a permanent apartment on West 83rd.

When I asked about Zemlinsky, Louise explained that he had suffered greatly with the stress and uncertainty, and his health had recently deteriorated significantly. A few months ago he had suffered a stroke, which had left him partially paralysed and he was also experiencing regular fainting spells. He could move only with great difficulty, confined to bed much of the time and unable to leave the apartment. They had read about the opening of the gallery in the press and he had asked her to enquire if I would pay him a visit as soon as was convenient.

A couple of days later, I left my apartment early in the morning and cut across Central Park, skirting the lake. An overnight winter storm had covered the paths and trees with a layer of white virgin snow. The tall skyscrapers surrounding the park reminded me of a vast castle wall enclosing an inner courtyard. The West Side was more run-down and neglected than the East Side, so apartments were cheaper. Even on such a bitterly cold morning, rough sleepers lay in doorways or gathered around burning oil drums, warming themselves by the flames.

I found the Zemlinskys' tenement block on West 83rd and went up to their apartment. Louise showed me in, thanking me for coming. Her husband was sat in his small bedroom at a table next to his bed. It was immediately obvious that the sharp-witted and energetic musician I had met nearly ten years ago in Landtmanns had gone, and in his place was a frail old man. His left hand was paralysed and his face twisted; he spoke deliberately, occasionally losing his train of thought. Despite appearing psychologically broken and physically spent, his power of memory still seemed fully intact.

'Thank you so much for coming to see me, Doktor Nirenstein,' he began. 'You must be very busy with your new gallery.'

'Not at all, it's my pleasure,' I replied. 'I have now adopted my mother's maiden name, Kallir, which I thought better suited to this new life. But I had no idea that you were in New York, and that we are almost neighbours! Your wife explained what a narrow escape you had in leaving Vienna.'

'It must have been even more difficult for you and your family. Louise says you didn't leave until a few months after the *Anschluss.* How did you manage that?'

'Fortunately, when the Gestapo came to our apartment and took away our passports, I asked for a receipt. So the next day I went along to the police station with the receipt and asked for them back! Coincidentally I knew the Chief of Police quite well, as he was a fellow stamp collector.'

Zemlinsky managed a weak smile.

'Just the same day I received a visit from my lawyer, Alfred Indra, warning me that warrants were being issued for our arrest.'

'Indra?' Zemlinsky repeated. 'He was my lawyer too! He leased our apartment, enabling us to leave. He also advised us to get out as quickly as we could.'

'That doesn't altogether surprise me', I replied. 'He did the same for Freud when he left for London. I actually suspect Indra may have been working for the Nazis and profiteering from his deals, especially when it came to the disposal of assets.'

'Nothing shocks me anymore, I'm sad to say, Herr Doktor', said Zemlinsky wearily. 'How is business here for you? Did you manage to bring your paintings with you?'

'I shipped them first to Paris and from Paris here. Amazingly they arrived before our furniture! Most are by Kokoschka but my recent exhibition of his work sold only one painting. It didn't help that *The New York Times* called his colours bilious and his work disturbing and unpalatable. I did also manage to extricate a few works by Klimt and Schiele, but so far American tastes seem quite provincial and decorative. I'm hoping for a better response in the new exhibition of French painting from the 19th and 20th century, which starts next week. A friend of my brother, a wealthy Jewish industrialist in Prague, has consigned to me some wonderful paintings by Van Gogh, Cézanne, Renoir and Manet.'

'What, if I might ask, has happened to your collection of paintings by Gerstl?' Zemlinsky enquired.

'They are still in Vienna, unfortunately, but safe under the care of my assistant, Vita Künstler. Perhaps one day, when this madness is all over, I will bring them here.'

Zemlinsky was already looking fatigued and was silent for a short time. Then he said:

'Herr Doktor, I have been thinking. There is something I would like to give you. When Louise was sorting out our belongings before we left, she came across a copy of Schott's first edition of Wagner's *Five Poems for a Female Voice*, inscribed inside with the initials 'RG'. I assume it must have been part of Mathilde's personal items. When she passed away, Schönberg had no desire to go through them and sent them all to me.'

'Gerstl gave her that book for her birthday. It is mentioned in a letter. The Wesendonck *Lieder* had a very special meaning for them both – another Richard and Mathilde!'

'That wasn't the only thing we found, Herr Doktor. Folded inside the jacket was this letter. It's not signed but I immediately recognised my sister's handwriting. It has no envelope, so I suppose it may never have been sent. Perhaps it will make more sense to you than it does to me.'

At that point Louise came in, clearly concerned for her husband.

'Alex', she said, 'you need to get back to bed. I'm sure Doktor Nirenstein will call to see you again'.

Taking that as my signal to leave, I said, 'I'd be delighted to come again. Please just call me or you're more than welcome to visit me in the gallery at any time.'

68 Liechtensteinstrasse

November 8th

Dearest Richard,

Last night I dreamt we were back on the Traunsee and I was searching for you. I was by the lake on the edge of the forest. The trees were tall and dark. The path and the water were lit by the moon. I was wearing a white summer dress with red roses though some had lost their petals. The warm night air was oppressive and there was a menacing silence. I became frightened because I couldn't make out the path in the stifling darkness. I started to sing so that you might hear me. I made my way forwards carefully in the inky blackness but suddenly I felt something crawling over my hands and face. A night bird screeched and there was a rustling sound above me. I began to run but tripped and fell. At first I thought it was a body but it was just a fallen tree trunk.

Eventually the path came out into a clearing and in the bright moonlight I could see it led back to the farmhouse with its white stone balcony and dark shutters. My dress was torn, my face and hands bleeding. I entered slowly, exhausted. There was no sound, not a breath of air. Still you weren't there. From the garden I saw the flickering lights of the houses across the lake. The moon had become pallid and there was not even the shadow of a night bird's wing in the clear sky.

I sat on a bench but my foot touched something hidden underneath. When I reached down to pull it out, my hand felt wet. It was covered in blood. Looking down, I saw your terrible ghost-like face. I thought that if I refused to look at it, it would just dissolve as in the forest. Maybe it was just the shadow of a tree or a trick of the moon. I turned back, hoping that it had gone. But it was still there – your skin, your eyes, your hair, your mouth. I called for help from the house but no-one came.

I tried to wake you. 'Please don't be dead', I cried. 'My darling, you can't be dead, I love you so much'. I took your cold hand and kissed it. I held it to my breast but it wouldn't get warm. Your blood was on my dress, on my face. The night was nearly gone, the night we were to spend together. I lay beside you but you wouldn't look at me. How frightening your staring eyes were! Why did they kill you? How dearly, how dearly I loved you. I have cut myself off from everything, and become a stranger to everyone but you. Since that very first time you took my hand, I have known nothing except you. Never before have I loved anyone so. Your smile, your words, your kiss, I loved them all so much.

Dawn broke on the mountains above the lake. There were low clouds in the sky lit by a pale yellow glow, shimmering like candlelight. What was I to do all alone, in this never-ending life, in this never-ending dream? The new morning separates us, always morning. How heavy your parting kiss! Another interminable day, waiting for the night. But now you will never wake again. A thousand people pass by but I don't recognise you among them. They are all alive with their eyes aflame but where are you? Suddenly it's dark again, your kiss like a beacon in my darkness, my lips burn and shine… towards you. You were there, I was searching.

34

Sometimes I wonder if I will ever see Vienna again. National Socialism and its apologists are destroying the values on which four hundred years of European civilisation have been built. The first visible symptom of the epidemic was a growing xenophobia – a primitive tribal instinct, a pathological suspicion and resentment towards outsiders – which is now in danger of sweeping across the world. Even if the Nazis are ultimately defeated, I ask myself why I would want to return and how I could live again among those friends and lifelong acquaintances that have been carried along, willingly or unwillingly, on a tide of blood and nationalism.

I remember driving from Vienna in the summer of 1937 to see the exhibition of 'Degenerate Art' staged in the arcades of the Munich Hofgarten. Almost every street, building and public space was covered with the red, clack and white emblem of the Swastika. I felt as if I had mistakenly stumbled into the annual convention of some mysterious, occult Society. Walking through The English Gardens I remembered Smaragda Berg's curious story about the fascination with mysticism, esoteric symbols and hidden codes shared by the new art movements and recognized a strange, disturbing parallel.

The exhibition had attracted over a million visitors in the first few weeks and the queue stretched far down the street. The paintings were packed in tightly and hung in a deliberately chaotic manner, surrounded by anti- Jewish and anti-Communist slogans pasted directly onto the wall: 'Madness becomes a method', 'Nature as seen by sick minds', 'Deliberate sabotage of German security'.

Adolf Ziegler, a favourite artist of Hitler, had been charged by Goebbels to lead a commission, whose task was to purge unacceptable art from German museums and many of them had been included in the exhibition. 'Come and judge for yourselves, German People!' Ziegler demanded at the opening. It was a Nazi referendum on modern art and in less than a year all modernist works would be purged from the German museums. In contrast, in the nearby House of German Art, the simultaneous Great German Art Exhibition glorified the traditional German Realism of the 19th century – in its most basic form, the way Hitler himself had painted. The 'Degenerate Art' exhibitions continued to pack in largely approving crowds in Berlin, Leipzig, Hamburg, Düsseldorf, Cologne as well as other cities throughout the country.

Although few artists were Jewish, an anti-Semitic film 'The Wandering Jew' was being played. 'We don't seek to make German culture suit the tastes of international Jewry', Hitler's voice blared out. 'It will be the cultural destruction of our people. An art which cannot count on the readiest and most heartfelt support of the great mass of the people but only upon the support of small cliques is intolerable.' Modernism was now foreign in every sense of the word. Expressionism was singled out for particular derision, even though ironically it was the most German of modern art movements. Influenced by psychologists such as Paul Julius Möbius and Max Nordau, whose popular book *Degeneration* equated biological degeneration with cultural decline, Expressionism was seen as a pathological condition, a symptom of mental illness. Nordau stated that degenerates are not always criminals, prostitutes, anarchists and lunatics but often authors and artists. Expressionist artists were described as facile daubers of paint and canvas smearers, who lacked national character.

Among the 650 works on show inevitably were a number of works by Kokoschka. While I stood in front of his prophetic painting *The Emigrants*, depicting the artist with two other haunted figures set against a blasted landscape, a voice with a thick Bavarian accent remarked jovially,

'Whoever painted that picture should be hung!' On my way home I resolved never to set foot on German soil again.

Here in America there is a strong mood to keep out of the war. Just the other day, Charles Lindbergh advocated that the US, like Stalin, should make a peace deal with Hitler, claiming it was the Jews who were driving America towards war. With my long-standing interest in aviation, I had been an admirer of Lindbergh for his exploits with the *Spirit of St Louis* until the day he accepted the Order of the German Eagle from Goering 'in the name of the Führer' -just weeks before *Kristallnacht*.. Lindbergh and his supporters believe that liberal democracy in Europe is finished and America should abandon its closest allies to their fate. 'America First' has become the motto in the popular press. One commentator said that refugees should be stopped from coming here because they will work for less and live on less, believing that they will put Americans out of work. 'America for Americans...Down with immigration forever', they say. Nobody thought to point out that virtually all Americans are immigrants.

The other face of the city is equally disturbing; so much conspicuous affluence and excessive luxury, yet so much open poverty. The metropolis is driven along twenty four hours a day at a relentless pace; the noise, traffic and blazing neon lights, the advertisements flashing on every street corner, the skyscrapers rising up like the spires of new cathedrals. I was reminded of Hitler's cynical remark that the masses are so stupid that they would believe anything you told them so long as it was expressed in the manner of an advertising slogan.

Yet most Americans seem obsessed by facts, the acquisition of any amount of selective unrelated information, demonstrated by the proliferation of radio quiz programs, which leads people to believe that knowledge is just a part of the entertainment industry, a competitive struggle for reward, rather than a private means of understanding the world they live in. Indeed it is very difficult to find any time for quiet reflection here. I miss the peace and silence of Vienna. Even the coffeehouses provide no refuge from the constant activity, no space for private contemplation or philosophical debate, no place to sit over a cup of coffee for hours, no refuge for those with nowhere to go. Never have Altenberg's lines seemed more prescient:

When you are worried or have problems of any kind – go to the coffee house! …
When you have four hundred crowns and spend five hundred – coffee house! …
When you can't find a lover – coffee house! …
When you feel like suicide – coffee house!

Memories, they say, live longer than dreams. Since the *Anschluss*, Austria no longer exists, swallowed up by the Greater German Reich. Austrian refugees have become stateless, our passports worthless; fugitives wandering from place to place, professional vagrants like Altenberg, citizens of everywhere and nowhere.

END

Milton Keynes UK
Ingram Content Group UK Ltd.
UKHW020728081123
432193UK00018B/694

9 781572 412231